Camp Club Girls

Elizabeth's
SAN ANTONIO SLEUTHING

Dedication

For all of my seventh-grade language arts students who
inspire me, delight me, and keep me on my toes.
And for Charis and Foster, who light up my life
and make my heart sing.

© 2011 by Barbour Publishing, Inc.

Edited by Jeanette Littleton.

ISBN 978-1-60260-402-5

Cover design: Thinkpen Design

Published by Barbour Publishing, Inc., P.O. Box 719, Uhrichsville, Ohio
44683, www.barbourbooks.com

*Our mission is to publish and distribute inspirational products offering
exceptional value and biblical encouragement to the masses.*

Member of the
Evangelical Christian
Publishers Association

Printed in the United States of America.
Dickinson Press Inc., Grand Rapids, MI 49512; December 2010; D10002608

Camp Club Girls

Elizabeth's
SAN ANTONIO SLEUTHING

Renae Brumbaugh

BARBOUR
PUBLISHING

CHAPTER 1

Trouble on the River

Splash! Fourteen-year-old Elizabeth gasped as cold water covered her face and clothes. She stood and shook the liquid from her blond hair and tried to wipe it from her clothes before it soaked through.

"Please remain in your seat at all times," the riverboat captain reminded her.

Didn't he see what just happened? Elizabeth's mother took her hand and gently pulled her back into her seat, helping Elizabeth brush the water off.

"What happened?" Elizabeth whispered, not wanting to interrupt the captain's tour speech. No one else seemed to notice her.

"It looks like a water balloon. I didn't see where it came from. We'll deal with it when the boat stops," her mother said. Elizabeth spied the small red piece of broken balloon at her feet.

"But who? Where?" Elizabeth looked at the tourists on the sidewalks. Surely no one would be brazen enough to throw a water balloon right out in the open. *The bridge!*

She looked behind her at the bridge they'd just passed. Empty.

Puzzled, she took the tissue her mother held out to her. Elizabeth's dad and brother were seated in front of her, and never even turned around. Apparently, no one else knew what had just happened.

Once again, she looked back at the bridge. This time, she saw three teenagers leaning over the other side. One was wearing a red cap and a plaid shirt. They were pointing and laughing at another riverboat making its way toward them.

Suspicious. Well, Mr. Red-cap. You haven't seen the last of me.

Elizabeth kept her eyes behind her, on the group of two boys and one girl, until a curve in the river blocked her view. Finally, she leaned back and tried to enjoy the rest of the ride.

When the riverboat pulled to the edge and the passengers were instructed to get off the boat, Robert Anderson turned and smiled at his daughter and wife. "I never get tired of San Antonio. As many times as I've ridden this riverboat and heard the same historical facts and the same corny jokes, I love it every time. Hey, what happened to you?" he asked Elizabeth, noticing her soaked hair.

"Some prankster dropped a water balloon on her," Sue Anderson spoke for her daughter. "It seemed to come out of nowhere."

"I saw who did it," said Elizabeth. "Or at least, who I think did it. Some teenagers were leaning over one of the bridges right after it happened."

Robert Anderson placed his hand on his daughter's shoulder and grinned. "I'm sorry, baby. That was a mean thing for someone to do. But if they were aiming for a pretty girl, I have to give them credit. Their aim was right on target."

Elizabeth crossed her arms. She didn't see the humor.

"Let's not jump to conclusions," said her dad as he helped her off the boat. "We'll go right now and talk to the captain. But just because you saw some kids on the bridge doesn't necessarily mean they're guilty."

Elizabeth nodded, but she wasn't convinced. She was going to be on the watch for that red ball cap and plaid shirt. She was so caught up in her thoughts, she wasn't even aware that the captain was talking to her. Suddenly, she realized he was asking her a question.

"Your parents just told me what happened, young lady. Did you see anything strange or suspicious?" the man repeated his question.

"Well, not really. Not right away. But when we got down the river a piece, I looked back to where it happened, and a group of teenagers was standing on the bridge. One of them was wearing a—"

"Did you see them with a water balloon?" the man interrupted her.

7

"No, but—"

The man shook his head. "I'm sorry, miss. Truly, I am. I had no idea. Sometimes people pull pranks on the tourists. But unless someone actually catches them in the act, we can't do much."

"I understand," Elizabeth told him. But that wasn't exactly true. She didn't understand why the man didn't tell local authorities and the sheriff's department and the CIA and the FBI and go on an all-out manhunt until those hoodlums were found, handcuffed, and thrown in the slammer.

Okay, maybe that's a little extreme, she thought. *But only a little.*

"Come on. Let's head back to the hotel and get you into some dry clothes. Or better yet, put on your swimsuit and we'll spend some time at the pool," said Mrs. Anderson, sensing her daughter's mood. "This time tomorrow, your friend Kate will be here."

Elizabeth brightened. "I can't wait! Kate is so cool—you'll love her. And she's bringing Biscuit, too. I'm glad Uncle Dan arranged for Biscuit to stay in the room with us."

She smiled at the thought of the scruffy little dog she and her sleuthing friends, the five other Camp Club Girls, had rescued at camp. "And I bet she'll bring tons of nifty little gadgets with her." *And maybe one of those gadgets will help me catch Mr. Red-cap and his friends.*

●—●—●

Later, Elizabeth lounged by the pool, sipping lemonade

from a large cup. She didn't appear to have a care in the world. But her mind was racing with thoughts of water balloons and red ball caps. Her cell phone startled her, beeping to indicate she had a new message.

It was Kate: JUST ARRIVED @ LITTLE ROCK. WHERE ARE YOU?

Elizabeth tried to think of where Little Rock was. *Oh, Arkansas!* she realized. *Only two states away!*

The phone beeped again.

Kate: YOU THERE?

Elizabeth smiled. She carefully texted back: RELAXING BY POOL IN SAN ANTONIO.

After a moment, Kate's reply came: DON'T HAVE TOO MUCH FUN. WAIT FOR ME. WE'LL ARRIVE IN OUR VAN AT 3 TOMORROW.

Elizabeth smiled. *Less than twenty-four hours and she'll be here, in the flesh!* She typed in: CAN'T WAIT!

A shadow covered her, and she looked up to find her mother. Taking the lounge chair beside her, Mrs. Anderson shook her head and laughed. "I'll never understand you kids and those text things. You have free long distance on that phone. Why don't you just make a phone call?"

Elizabeth laughed, too. "I guess that would make more sense. But texting is fun. Kind of like reading code."

Mrs. Anderson leaned back in her chair and flipped open a magazine. "To each her own," she said. "By the way, there's a puppet show this evening at the Fiesta Noche del Rio. Your father and I are taking James to it. You're welcome to come, but since Uncle Dan will be on duty, you can stay here if you want."

"Thanks, Mom. I'll think about it," Elizabeth said, reaching for her lemonade. She sipped the cool drink then leaned back and closed her eyes. She was almost asleep when she gasped, covered in cold water for the second time that day.

James giggled and continued splashing her from the pool. "Come in the water with me, Betty-boo!" he taunted.

"I told you to stop calling me that!" she demanded. A moment later, she was in the pool with her little brother, splashing and laughing at his antics.

"Cannonball!" Mr. Anderson yelled out just before hitting the water with a gigantic splash.

"Oh Robert! You got me all wet!" cried Mrs. Anderson. "I guess I'll have to climb in there, too, just to protect myself."

The Andersons spent the rest of the afternoon splashing in the pool. When they left the pool for dinner, they were famished.

●—●—●

Elizabeth pushed back from the table at the riverside café and eyed the pile of corn husks on her plate. "Those were the best tamales I've ever tasted," she said.

"You say that every time we eat here," Mr. Anderson reminded his daughter, his eyes twinkling.

"It's true. I'm glad we come to San Antonio often.

Maybe someday we can convince the chef to give us the recipe," she replied.

Mrs. Anderson laughed. "Oh, I think it will take more than the recipe to duplicate those tamales. It takes years of practice to learn to cook like that."

"Well, I'm young. I can learn. I'll practice as much as it takes, if it means I can have these tamales anytime I want them," Elizabeth said.

"Here, Beth. You can have the rest of mine. I'm full," said James.

Elizabeth groaned. She was stuffed, too. But she couldn't turn down more tamales.

Mrs. Anderson watched her daughter take another bite and laughed. "Well, at least I know how to make you eat. Normally, you don't eat enough to feed a bird."

Elizabeth put down her fork. "I can't do it. I love these things, but I just don't have room for another bite," she said. "If you don't mind, I think I'll skip the puppet show. I'm going back to the hotel to lie down. Maybe watch television."

"Okay," her father said. "Just be sure to check in with Uncle Dan. If you need anything, you know he'll be at the front desk. We'll be there in about an hour."

"Yes, sir," Elizabeth replied, and stood to her feet. "I'll see you in a little while."

Ambling back to the hotel, she watched for signs of that red ball cap. She saw tourists of all shapes, sizes, and ages, but no gangs of laughing teenagers.

Oh well, she thought. *There's always tomorrow. And tomorrow, Kate will be here to help me.*

"Howdy, Elizabeth," called Uncle Dan when she stepped into the lobby.

"Hi," she said, walking over and leaning against the desk.

"Where is the rest of the Anderson clan?" he asked, rolling his wheelchair so he could look directly at her.

"They're going to see a puppet show. I'm headed upstairs to chill out for a while."

"Okay. Have fun. You know where I am if you need me," he said.

With a wave, Elizabeth walked to the glass-walled elevator and pushed the button. One side of the elevator offered a view of the Riverwalk, and Elizabeth enjoyed looking out on her way to the fourth floor.

Maybe I'll just ride up and down the elevator for a while, she thought.

She pushed the button for the top floor, even though her room was on the fourth. She pressed her nose against the glass as she rode to the highest point of the hotel. The elevator stopped and opened its doors, waiting for her to exit.

Instead, she stood, still looking out the glass at the view of tourists and riverboats, restaurants and mariachi bands. To her left, she saw the Fiesta Noche del Rio, and after a few moments, identified her parents and brother. James was bouncing up and down, clapping for the puppets. Elizabeth smiled. He wasn't bad, as far as brothers were concerned.

Shifting her gaze to the right, she counted the little stone bridges up and down the Riverwalk. These bridges were located at different places along the Riverwalk so people could easily cross the narrow man-made river. Restaurants and souvenir shops lined both sides of the river. Elizabeth watched a family pose for a picture on the steps of one of the bridges.

She looked on to the next bridge, still counting. *Three, four, five. . .what's going on there?* She noticed a commotion on one of the bridges. *Why are those people ducking down on the bridge?Are they trying to hide from the people below? And was that—*It was! A plaid shirt! But no ball cap.

Wait! There it was. The boy in the middle, who was about the size of an ant from her vantage point, pulled something red out of his back pocket and placed it on his head.

The group of two boys and one girl stood up. Mr. Red-cap pointed at a riverboat in the distance, and the others appeared to be laughing.

That's them! she thought. *Those are the ones who dropped the water balloon on my head! Well, they're not going to get away with it.*

She whipped around and pressed the button for the ground floor. Keeping her eyes on the group of teenagers, she went down, down, down and waited for the doors to open.

When the elevator stopped on the ground floor, Elizabeth pressed against the doors, willing them to open. Funny, she hadn't noticed the doors being this slow before. When the doors opened, she took off running through the lobby.

"Whoa! Beth! Where's the fire?" asked Uncle Dan as she whizzed past the front desk.

"Can't talk now. I'll explain when I get back," she called, and continued through the ornate doors to the Riverwalk.

Outside, she looked around to get her bearings. The bridge where she saw the teenagers was. . .this way. She dodged tourists as she dashed to the bridge. She took the steps two at a time, but when she reached the top, no one was there.

Where did they go?

Looking this way and that, she only saw a sea of tourists. To one side, a mariachi band played an upbeat song, and people clapped in time to the music. Scanning the crowds, she looked for that red cap. If he wasn't wearing it, she had no hope of finding the group.

Finally, she saw them seated at a riverside café table, munching on tortilla chips.

The nerve! she thought. *They're just sitting there enjoying the Riverwalk, as innocent as lambs! Well, they won't get away with this.*

Elizabeth walked down the stone steps and in the direction of the little group. She smiled sweetly at the waiter and sat at a table a few feet from the threesome. She pretended to study her menu, while straining to hear their conversation.

"One of these days, you'll get caught, you know," said the girl.

Red-cap Boy, whose cap was now hanging out of his back pocket, stretched his legs out from under the table and smiled. "Aww, we're not hurting anybody. People should expect to get a little wet at the Riverwalk."

The girl shook her head. "Well, from now on, when you pull your little stunts, I'm leaving. I don't want to get grouped in with you and your shenanigans."

Red-cap Boy laughed and said something in Spanish.

The girl said, "What do you mean, you won't get caught? You don't know that."

Elizabeth peeked out from behind her menu and saw Red-cap smiling. His white teeth, framed by two deep dimples, stood out against his creamy brown skin. "Even if we do get caught, what will they do to us? We're not breaking any laws. Besides, who would convict this face?" He gave the girl a cocky smile.

Why, that conceited little criminal! thought Elizabeth. *You really think you're something special, don't you? Well, Mr. Red-cap, you just wait. We'll see who's smiling when your gig is up. And trust me, your gig will be up very soon.*

The threesome pushed back from the table and began to leave just as Elizabeth's waiter returned to take her order. "What can I get for you, miss?" he asked.

Thinking quickly, she said, "You know, I don't think I'll eat right now after all. Sorry to have troubled you." She excused herself and followed the group at a distance.

Through the crowds she went, keeping her eyes glued to that red cap. She almost didn't see the rolling hot dog cart until it was too late. Scooting aside at the last moment, she said, "Oh, excuse me, sir."

The old man smiled. "No problem, miss. Would you care for a hot dog?"

"No, thank you," she said politely and moved forward. But it was too late. The red cap was nowhere in sight.

Elizabeth turned and made her way back to the hotel. *You may have escaped me today, buddy, but just wait until tomorrow. . . .*

CHAPTER 2

Breakdown!

Mr. Anderson woke up his family bright and early, and they spent the better part of the morning at the Tower of the Americas, a 750-foot-tall tower with a revolving restaurant at the top. As they left the tower, he said, "I love the view from the top! Too bad the restaurant wasn't open yet. Let's take another riverboat ride, then get some lunch. I never get tired of riding those little boats!"

Now, as Elizabeth sat in a River City Cruise boat watching the bridges and sidewalks for any signs of the boy with the red cap, she heard a strange noise.

Pu–pu–pu–put, puput, pu–pu. . .rrrrrr. . .rrrrrr. . .pu. . . put. . .pu. The engine of the small riverboat groaned and sputtered. Then it died, as concerned tourists looked at each other in confusion.

"That's nice. I fork out ten bucks to ride this heap of junk, and now we're stranded," called a tall, thin, middle-aged man from the back of the boat.

"I'm very sorry for the inconvenience, folks," replied the frustrated boat captain. "All of your money will be refunded, as soon as I push this boat to shore. Just report to the ticket office and tell them what happened."

Elizabeth felt sorry for the captain. The crowd gasped in surprise as he suddenly jumped overboard! Their surprise turned to laughter, however, as he stood up. The water of the famous San Antonio Riverwalk only came to the man's waist.

Another riverboat passed but didn't stop to help. Its captain looked long and hard at the stranded group. The man leaned forward, one foot propped on the boat's railing, and the sun glinted off his polished shoe.

Is he smiling? thought Elizabeth. *Why doesn't he offer to help us?* She noticed the competing company's logo on the side of the boat—Santa Anna Tours. *Maybe they have rules about helping the competition or something. . . .*

"Here, let me give you a hand," said Elizabeth's father, leaping into the water. Together, the two men pushed the boat to the edge of the water and secured it to the cement siding with ropes.

The riverboat captain hefted himself onto the sidewalk then held out a hand to help Mr. Anderson. "Thank you, sir. I'll make sure your family gets free rides for the rest of your visit here in San Antonio."

"That won't be necessary," said Robert Anderson. "I was happy to help."

The captain helped his passengers disembark. The tall, grumbly man from the back row stepped off. In a loud voice, he said, "I'd rather have a refund than a free ride. From now on, I'll take my business to Santa Anna Tours. Now *that's* a boat you can count on."

The rude man walked away, continuing his tirade as he went. The riverboat captain kept a polite smile pasted on his face, but Elizabeth wasn't fooled. The man was concerned about his business.

"Hey, can I jump in before I get out?" asked James. Elizabeth's little brother loved an adventure. And he loved to get wet.

"No, you can't," replied Sue Anderson, helping the six-year-old off the boat. "One wet male in the family is enough for now."

Elizabeth helped her mother step across to the sidewalk. "I'll go swimming with you when we get back to the hotel," she told James. Moving close to her father, she listened to the conversation between him and the captain.

"I don't understand what could have happened," the man said. "We service the motors every week. But this is the third time this has happened in two weeks!"

"That is strange," replied Elizabeth's dad. "Who services your boats? Perhaps they've started doing something different . . .ordering parts from a new company or something."

"Maybe so. . . ," said the man. "Thank you again for your help."

"No problem," replied Elizabeth's dad. He was sopping wet from the waist down, and he looked pretty funny. "Let's go eat Mexican food!" he said to his family.

"Uh, Dad? Don't you think you should get into some dry clothes first?" Elizabeth asked.

"Nonsense. In this Texas heat, I'll be dry in no time. And besides, I'm starved!" He led his family the few steps to the closest outdoor café, the Rio Rio. The Riverwalk was lined with restaurants, and the Andersons had decided to eat at every one. The host seated them at a table bordering the water.

Elizabeth's family studied their menus, discussing which new dish to try, but Elizabeth wasn't interested in food. Looking at her watch, she said, "In two more hours I'm going to see Kate!"

●—●—●

A couple of hours later, Elizabeth sat in the ornate lobby of the plush hotel. The Andersons could never have afforded such luxury if Uncle Dan hadn't gotten them a discount. He had also helped Kate's youth group get a good rate for their San Antonio mission trip.

Pulling the letter—actually an e-mail that Elizabeth had printed—from her pocket, she unfolded it. It was wrinkled and smudged from all the times Elizabeth had read it during the past few weeks.

Dear Elizabeth,
I'm coming to Texas! My church youth group
is planning a mission trip to the San Antonio

Riverwalk, and they're letting me come along. I have always wanted to see Texas.

How close are you to San Antonio? Do you think you could meet me there? I would love to see you again. Since it doesn't look like you'll come to Philadelphia any time soon, maybe this will work.

We are still in the planning stages of the mission trip. I'm not sure where we'll stay yet. Let me know if you think you can meet me there. You have to come. You just have to!

I'll talk to you soon. Biscuit sends kisses.

Love,
Kate

Elizabeth smiled as she refolded the letter. San Antonio was one of the Andersons' favorite getaway places! Within two weeks after Elizabeth received the letter, Uncle Dan had helped Kate's youth minister make all the arrangements. And now, the youth group from Kate's church would be here any minute! She watched out the front windows of the lobby, looking for a church van from Philadelphia.

"A watched pot never boils," said a voice from behind her.

"Hi, Uncle Dan. I can't help it! I can't wait to see Kate!" Elizabeth told him.

"I heard you had an exciting morning at the Riverwalk," he said.

21

"Yeah, it was the strangest thing! We were puttering along listening to the captain tell stories and point out the sights when the motor just died!"

Uncle Dan looked concerned. "The owner of that riverboat company is a friend of mine. That's been happening a lot lately, and it's not good for his business."

"I sure hope they fix the problem so— They're here!" Elizabeth jumped up as she saw the blue church van pull into the parking lot. Rushing through the ornate doors, she stopped herself before running into the flow of traffic.

"Maybe you should wait here for her," said Uncle Dan, following her.

Soon, the van doors opened, and teenaged boys and girls climbed out. One by one, Elizabeth watched each new person. *No Kate. No Kate. Where is Kate?* The group of teens approached the lobby, laughing and talking. Some of them smiled politely at Elizabeth.

Suddenly, like the parting of the Red Sea, they started moving to either side as a blond wisp of a girl with black-framed glasses pushed through. "Excuse me! Pardon me, coming through! I've got to find my friend. . .Elizabeth!"

Kate dropped her bags and dashed to Elizabeth. "Oh, am I ever glad to see you! That was one long trip. But I'm finally here! And you're here!"

Suddenly, Kate's backpack began barking.

"Biscuit!" shouted Elizabeth. "Wow, Kate, I can't believe you're both here at last! We are going to have so much fun!"

She hugged her friend, then helped free the wiggling dog.

"Biscuit, did you ride the whole way in that backpack?" Elizabeth stroked the small dog's black and white fur while fighting off slobbery puppy kisses.

"He slept most of the way," said Kate. "I'm so glad your uncle said I could bring him. He's missed you, Elizabeth! And so have I."

A twentysomething man approached and said, "You must be Elizabeth. Kate has talked of nothing else for the entire trip. I'm Gary, Kate's youth minister."

Elizabeth shook the man's hand. He said, "Kate, we'll be on the fifth floor if you need us."

"Thanks, Gary," she said, and the two girls gathered Kate's backpack and suitcase and headed for the elevator.

Biscuit, on the other hand, gave a series of excited barks. "Maybe we'd better find a patch of grass first, so Biscuit can take care of business," said Kate.

Both girls laughed, and Kate clipped a leash onto the dog's collar. Uncle Dan pointed them toward the back door, which led to a small courtyard. Within minutes, they were on their way to the Andersons' room on the fourth floor.

"I can't wait to tell you what happened this morning," Elizabeth told her friend.

"I can't wait to see the Riverwalk! And the Alamo! And the Tower of the Americas! How soon can we get started?" asked Kate.

"Whoa, there! Slow down, tourist. We have plenty of time. We don't have to see everything today. Why don't we start by getting your things unpacked? Then we'll head to the Riverwalk. Are you hungry? The food here is great," Elizabeth said.

Kate gave her a comical look. "What do you mean, 'Am I hungry?' I'm always hungry!"

Elizabeth's parents were in the suite when the girls arrived. The room was set up with two bedrooms—one for Mr. and Mrs. Anderson, and one for Kate and Elizabeth. James slept on the pull-out sofa in the living room.

"Wow, this place sure is fancy. I've never stayed in a hotel this nice!" exclaimed Kate.

"Neither have we." Elizabeth laughed. "It's one of the perks of having an uncle who works here. Mom, Dad, I'd like you to meet Kate. Kate, this is my mom and dad, Robert and Sue Anderson."

"It's very nice to meet you both," said Kate, reaching to shake their hands.

Suddenly Biscuit growled. Something was moving under the kitchen table. The chairs shifted, and James crawled out. Biscuit decided the moving boy wasn't a threat, and began wagging his tail.

"This is my little brother, James," continued Elizabeth.

James waved, but kept his eyes on Biscuit. "Can I pet him?" he asked.

As if to answer the question, Biscuit jumped on James

and began licking his face. James fell over, giggling, but Biscuit showed no signs of letting up.

"It looks like those two will be fast friends," Kate said.

Elizabeth picked up Kate's bags and said, "Come on. I'll show you our room."

The two headed into their bedroom, and Kate flopped on the bed. "This will be so much fun. I'm so glad you and your family could come."

"San Antonio is one of our favorite places. We come here a lot, but we usually stay at a discount motel. Now that Uncle Dan's working at this hotel, we'll probably visit even more."

Kate unzipped her suitcase and pulled out her laptop. "I need to set up my computer. I haven't been able to update my blog or check the comments in two days! Oh, hey, check out my new business card." She handed Elizabeth a small card that read:

SUPER SLEUTHS, INC.
KATE OLIVER, SUPER SLEUTH
HTTP://SUPERSLEUTHSINC.BLOGSPOT.COM/
FOR ANSWERS TO ALL YOUR SLEUTHING QUESTIONS!

"Cool!" said Elizabeth. "Bring a handful of them with you to the Riverwalk. You can pass them out."

"Good idea," said Kate as she plugged in her small computer.

Elizabeth glanced into the open suitcase and had to laugh. Only a few clothes were in the suitcase. Most of it was packed with electronic gadgets and doodads.

Kate's fingers began to fly as she punched in her blog's address and logged in with her password. "Hooray! I have six comments!" she exclaimed.

Elizabeth looked over Kate's shoulder as she began responding to each one. "Your blog is really getting popular. Besides the comment from Bailey, the rest are from people I've never heard of."

Kate smiled. "Two of them are from my cousins. But the other three are from strangers. My blog is getting famous!"

"Well, hurry up. I want to hear about all these gadgets you brought. And I'm eager to show you the Riverwalk," Elizabeth told her.

"Most of these comments are just telling me they like my blog. It's more fun when I get actual questions to answer. But hey, I'm not complaining." She finished typing her last response, then turned her attention to her suitcase. "A lot of these are the same ones I had when we were at camp together. But here's a new one. It's a bug."

"A bug?" Elizabeth asked, crinkling her nose.

"Yeah, you know. Like the spies use. You can hide it and listen. It's better than the one we used on Biscuit's collar at camp. Instead of recording, we can actually listen as the conversation is taking place."

"Oh, kind of like a walkie-talkie?" asked Elizabeth.

"Well, sort of. Picture those police shows, where the police hide outside the house in a van, listening to the bad guys' conversation. This is what they use."

Elizabeth's eyes widened as she held the tiny tool. "Whoa," she whispered. "This is too cool."

Kate held out another small device. "This is a tracker. Why don't you put it on your phone while I'm here, to keep from losing it. During the trip, I had it on Biscuit's collar, in case we got separated."

"That's a good idea," said Elizabeth, slipping the device on her phone. "So, are you ready to go?"

"Yep," Kate said, and the girls headed to the living room.

"Mom, Dad, can we roam around the Riverwalk for a little while?" asked Elizabeth.

"Yes, but don't go past the Fiesta Noche. The time now is two forty-five. Take your cell phone and check in with us in an hour. Plan to meet us in the lobby at five o'clock for dinner," said Mrs. Anderson.

Kate slipped the leash around Biscuit's neck and attached the small tracker to his collar. With a wave, the two girls headed out the door.

In the lobby, the girls pushed open the heavy glass doors that led to the Riverwalk. Outside, Kate adjusted her glasses. "Whoa! This is so cool. It's even better than the pictures! Here, hold this," she said, handing Biscuit's leash to Elizabeth. She rummaged through her backpack and pulled out her camera phone. "Smile!" she said, and snapped a picture of Elizabeth kneeling next to Biscuit. A riverboat rumbled past in the background.

Kate then pulled out her cell phone and dialed a number.

"Who are you calling?" Elizabeth asked.

"My parents. They told me to call them as soon as I arrived, but I got so excited, I forgot."

There was an answer at the other end of the line, and Kate began talking to her mother. Elizabeth walked with Biscuit to the water's edge, taking in the scenery. Soon, she heard a familiar *pa–pa–pa–put. . .rrrr. . .rrrr. . .pa–pa–put.* Looking to her left, she could see that once again, a River City Cruise boat had died.

Kate hung up the phone and said, "What are we waiting for? Let's go!" Then, noticing Elizabeth's concerned look, she said, "What's wrong?"

"Oh, another riverboat just died. Let me tell you what happened to us this morning."

The two girls walked toward one of the stone bridges while Elizabeth relayed the story.

"Maybe we should use a different riverboat company, if we ride at all. I'm not sure I want to end up in a dead boat!" Kate responded.

"Maybe," Elizabeth said. "I just think it's strange. My family has been to this Riverwalk many times, and we ride the boats every time. This has never happened before. Now, all of a sudden, riverboats are dying all over the place!"

Another boat puttered by, this one from Santa Anna Tours. The girls watched as the new boat moved past the stalled boat without even offering help. This time, they could hear its captain make a joke about the stalled boat, and the passengers laughed.

"I guess you folks chose the right boat to ride," said the captain of the working boat.

Biscuit pulled away from Elizabeth and barked. A bird had landed just feet from him, and was pecking on a tortilla chip someone had dropped. With one last look at the boats, the girls tugged on Biscuit's leash and headed in the opposite direction.

"Come on," said Kate. "I'm starved."

"Okay! Let's go over this bridge. The restaurant on the other side serves the best tortilla chips and salsa you've ever tast—"

Elizabeth stopped short as they reached the top of the stone bridge. A group of teenagers stood there, pointing and laughing at the stalled boat, and shouting things in Spanish.

And right in the middle of them was the boy with the red cap.

Kate and Elizabeth on Duty!

"Come with me," Elizabeth said, grabbing Kate's arm and dragging the girl behind her.

"Whoa, what's the rush?" Kate asked, doing her best to keep up.

The group hushed as Elizabeth, Kate, and Biscuit appeared, but barely gave them room to pass. One of them smiled at Biscuit, who barked in return.

"Easy, little guy. I'm not going to hurt you," the boy said.

Elizabeth kept moving. She wanted to stay close, but she wasn't ready to talk to her suspects yet. As soon as the girls and Biscuit were descending the stairs on the other side, the group started talking again. Biscuit resisted Kate's lead and continued barking at the group.

"Biscuit, cut that out!" she scolded. Finally, the little dog obeyed.

Elizabeth led Kate to a nearby café and found an empty table. The waiter immediately placed a basket of tortilla chips and a bowl of salsa in front of them. "Cool!" said Kate. "Now that's what I call service! Now, do you want to tell me what that was about?"

Elizabeth leaned forward and motioned toward the group, which was still standing on the bridge. "I haven't told you about the water balloon." Over chips and salsa, she explained the whole story to her friend.

"Aha! A mystery to solve. Never fear, Elizabeth, my dear. I have everything we could possibly need to catch those guys. And when they're caught, we'll throw the book at them!"

Elizabeth giggled at Kate's enthusiasm. *Yep. Those guys don't know what they're in for,* she thought.

They continued munching and chatting about their plans.

"Gary wants me to help with the Bible club every day. I told him you'd probably want to help, too."

"That sounds like fun. What will you be doing?" Elizabeth asked, keeping an eye on the group, which had now moved to a café on the other side of the bridge. She had a clear view of them from her spot.

"It's supposed to be right here on the Riverwalk somewhere. Something about a little church in a plaza or something? We're going to do a Bible club for kids and hopefully draw in some of the locals. Apparently, a lot of kids hang out at the Riverwalk, and we're going to try to get them involved."

"Sounds like a good idea to me. It's probably at the Little Church at La Villita. It's a historic landmark, but also an active church."

Just then, Biscuit wagged his tail and pulled against his leash, which was attached to Kate's chair. A little girl in a pink dress walked by, holding her mother's hand. She looked about four years old. Large brown eyes peeked through brown curls that cascaded down her cheeks and covered most of her face. When she noticed Elizabeth and Kate looking at her, she buried her face in her mother's skirt. The two continued on their way.

Biscuit barked a friendly yap and settled back beneath Kate's chair. "Biscuit loves children," Kate said. "That's one of the reasons Gary let me bring him. He hopes Biscuit will attract kids to the Bible club. Oh look! There's Gary now!"

Kate's youth minister and several teenagers were headed toward the girls. "Hey there, Kate! Are you having fun yet?" Gary asked.

"You'd better believe it! And Biscuit is already drawing attention."

"Good," said the man. "Don't forget, our mime troupe is performing at seven p.m. at the Fiesta Noche del Rio—it's a little theater area right here on the Riverwalk. Elizabeth, I hope you'll help us out this week. Kate tells me you're a real firecracker when it comes to ministry work."

Elizabeth blushed. "I don't know about that. . . ," she replied.

"Don't let her fool you. She plays the piano, sings, and has over half of the Bible memorized," Kate said.

"I do not," Elizabeth said, laughing.

Gary smiled. "Well, you'll be a great addition to our team. You two have fun, and I'll see you both at seven o'clock." He followed the teenagers into a T-shirt shop.

Elizabeth waved good-bye then looked across the river to find the group of teens. They were gone.

●——●——●

Later that evening, Kate groaned. Mr. and Mrs. Anderson had treated the girls to a huge plate of the gooiest, cheesiest burritos Kate had ever eaten. "I'm stuffed," she said.

"Would you like some sopapillas?" asked the waitress, and the Andersons laughed. "Maybe later," Mr. Anderson said.

"It's six forty-five," Elizabeth said, looking at her watch. "Why don't we go on over to the Fiesta Noche and try to get good seats. I can't wait to see your youth group perform," she told Kate.

"We'll all go," said Mrs. Anderson. "But we'll meet you girls there. I want to walk around for a few minutes."

Kate and Elizabeth waved good-bye and headed toward the Fiesta Noche. When they arrived they were surprised to see the red-cap boy and his friends. They were sprawled out in the center of the seating area, talking and laughing loudly. In Spanish. Elizabeth caught a few of the words, but her Spanish was rusty.

When the teens saw the girls and Biscuit, they started talking about the *perro*. Elizabeth knew they were referring to Biscuit. The little dog strained his leash and barked. Red-cap Boy said something the group thought was hilarious.

Elizabeth and Kate looked at each other and took seats a few rows in front of the group. "Maybe we'll overhear them admit to something," whispered Kate. Biscuit watched the teenagers. He continued to softly growl.

"No, Biscuit. Stop that!" said Kate, and the dog calmed a bit. But his ears remained stiff.

The two girls tried to focus on the stage. "This is so cool!" said Kate. "I've never seen anything like this! The river runs between the stage and the audience. I guess they don't have to worry about anyone rushing the stage."

Elizabeth laughed. "I guess not. They're pretty safe over there, unless one of them falls in the water!"

A door at the back of the stage opened, and two girls from Kate's youth group stepped out. "Hi, Kate! Do you guys want to help us? You can cross at the bridge and come to the back if you want."

The two girls stood, Biscuit in tow, and retraced their path to the bridge. Just as they were about to cross they saw the Andersons.

"Where are you going? I thought the show was about to start," asked Sue Anderson.

"We've been asked to help," Elizabeth told her mother.

Mrs. Anderson smiled. "That sounds like fun. We'll be in the audience. We'll meet you at the seating area after the performance."

Elizabeth, Kate, and Biscuit hurried across the bridge and through the back door of the stage area. Gary greeted them with a smile. "Hi, girls! You're just in time. Most of our people are in costume, and we don't want them to go onto the stage until the show starts. Could you two wheel this box of props out there? Just put the box by the back wall and come right back."

"No problem," replied Elizabeth.

Kate wasn't sure what to do with Biscuit, so Elizabeth took the small dog and placed him inside the box.

The two girls pushed the heavy box on wheels to the stage area. The seats were filling up, and Elizabeth waved at her parents.

"Look! It's Beth!" shouted James.

Suddenly, Elizabeth lost her footing and fell on her backside. Center stage. Red-cap, having heard James call her name, started laughing. "Way to go, Beth!" he called.

Why, the nerve of that boy! she thought. *I'll show him!* Instead of being embarrassed, she decided to play up her public disaster. Standing to her feet, she faced the audience and took a grand bow.

Red-cap hooted with laughter, and the audience cheered. She kept bowing until Kate ran out and grabbed her, pulling her, smiling and waving, off the stage.

"What was that about?" asked Kate with a laugh. "What happened to the girl who doesn't like to be on stage?"

"I never said I don't like to be on stage," Elizabeth countered. "I said I don't like to play the piano or sing in front of others. Falling and looking like an idiot? I can handle that just fine."

Gary and the others in the youth group laughed and patted Elizabeth on the back. "Good job, girls. You can head back over and sit in the audience now, if you want."

"Okay," said Elizabeth, realizing they wouldn't be able to see much of the show from backstage.

They were halfway across the bridge when Kate stopped. "Biscuit!" she cried. "We left him in the box!"

The girls saw that the performers were already walking onto the stage. Wide-eyed, they looked at each other.

"What will we do?" asked Elizabeth.

"I don't know. I guess we can't do anything except watch and see what happens!"

The two girls quickly went to the seating area and sat down. The performers had white painted faces and began presenting a mime. Music played in the background as the main character mimed being lost. His facial expressions were comical, and the audience laughed at all the right times.

However, Elizabeth and Kate watched the box at the back of the stage. At any moment, they expected Biscuit to leap out and make his grand stage debut.

*Pa–pa–pa–put! Rrrrr. . .rrrrrrr. . .pa–pa put. . .rrrrrrr. . . rrrr. . .rrrrr. . .*The audience's attention turned to the riverboat coming around the bend. This time, however, the boat seemed out of control, and was headed straight for the stage, straight for the performers!

Boom! The boat banged into the platform. The passengers on the boat gasped and clung to the sides. Fortunately, it wasn't going fast enough for anyone to fall overboard.

It did, however, cause quite a stir on the stage. The performers backed away from the boat, and one of the mimes landed in the box where Biscuit was! They heard a loud yelp, and then saw Biscuit wiggling out of the box! He leaped onto the stage, causing even more excitement among the mimes.

Biscuit ran this way, then that on the stage, not knowing how to escape. Kate yelled, "Biscuit! It's okay, boy! Calm down!"

Hearing his beloved owner's voice, he searched the crowd for her. Spotting her across the river, he didn't even hesitate. He splashed right into the water and swam to the other side, while people cheered and clapped. The riverboat captain looked frustrated, his passengers looked confused, and the audience wondered if it was all part of the show!

Reaching the other side, Biscuit climbed out, shaking water onto the entire front row and leaving them squealing. The little dog lunged through the audience, leaving wet, muddy paw prints in his wake, and flew into Kate's arms.

"Hey, cut that out," Kate cried as he covered her with drippy kisses. He transferred his messy love to Elizabeth for a moment, then back to Kate. Before long, the audience began applauding, as if they had enjoyed the show.

Gary came onto the stage and announced, "Hello, folks! As you can see, we are having some technical difficulties. Just hold tight, and we'll start our performance again in a few minutes."

He then helped the riverboat captain onto the stage. Together, they helped the boat's occupants onto the stage and out the back door.

Elizabeth heard snickering behind her. She turned to see Red-cap pointing and laughing at the riverboat captain, just as he and his friends had done earlier in the day.

"I wonder what could be causing so many of the boats to break down," she said.

"It's a mystery to me," Kate replied. "Maybe we should investigate. This sounds like a job for the. . ." She paused, waiting for Elizabeth to chime in.

"Camp Club Girls!" they said together, then laughed.

"Why do we find mysteries everywhere we go?" asked Elizabeth.

"It's almost as if the mysteries find us," said Kate.

Elizabeth began speaking under her breath.

"What? I can't hear you," said Kate.

Elizabeth laughed. "I just thought of a mystery verse. 'God has chosen to make known among the Gentiles the glorious riches of this mystery, which is Christ in you, the hope of glory.' It's in Colossians 1:27."

Kate just stared at her friend. "How do you do that? You know a verse for everything."

"Well, I wish I were half as good at figuring out all those gadgets you carry around with you."

Kate laughed. "I guess we can't all be good at everything. But at least we're both good at solving mysteries. And I have a feeling this will be a tough one."

The girls leaned back as the mimes made their second entry onto the stage. Yep. This was going to be a tough one, all right.

●—●—●

Later that night, Elizabeth looked over Kate's shoulder as she typed onto her blog:

Hypothetical Mystery Challenge:
A taxi company that has always been reliable suddenly begins to experience difficulties. All over town, the taxi motors begin dying, even though the cars are serviced weekly. The company's reputation suffers.
Who or what might be responsible?

"That's a really good idea, Kate!" said Elizabeth, patting her friend on the shoulder.

Kate smiled with satisfaction. "From time to time, I write a pretend mystery for my readers to solve. Little do they know, the mysteries are real. I just change enough details so no one will figure it out."

"What a clever way to get some outside help. Now, let's

send out an SOS to the other Camp Club Girls. They're sure to help us figure it out. I don't even know where to start."

Kate typed the whole story, including the riverboat mishap, Elizabeth's water balloon experience, and the teenaged troublemakers. In the subject line, she wrote: *New Mystery! Need Help!*

She continued on, typing what she and Elizabeth had seen so far. Just a couple of minutes after she pressed SEND, Elizabeth's cell phone rang. It was Sydney.

"Hey, Beth. I just read the e-mail. Tell Kate she'd better learn to swim if she's going to solve a river mystery."

Kate, who was standing close enough to the phone to hear, responded, "Ha, ha. Very funny. I plan to stay on dry land for this mystery, thank you very much."

Elizabeth and Sydney laughed. Kate was brilliant. Nearly a genius. But an athlete, she was not.

"We don't even know where to start. Do you have any suggestions?" Elizabeth asked Sydney.

"Well, those teenagers sound suspicious to me. You said they were laughing and pointing at the boats? It doesn't seem funny. Maybe they had something to do with it."

"That's what I'm thinking," said Elizabeth.

"Well, keep me posted. And tell Kate not to fall in." With a quick good-bye, Sydney hung up.

Checking the computer screen, they saw two more e-mails had come in. One was from Bailey:

Nail the teenagers! Follow their every move. I'll bet they are the guilty parties.

The next was from McKenzie:

Are there any competing riverboat companies?

Elizabeth and Kate looked at each other.

"There is that other company that never stops to help. I wonder if they are trying to drum up more business for themselves," Elizabeth mused.

"That's a definite possibility. I wonder what Miss Hollywood is going to suggest." As if on cue, Alex's user name popped up on the live chat page.

> Alex: *Oh, this is soooo Nancy Drew! I wish I were there with you all.*
>
> Kate: *We wish you were here, too. Any ideas about the first step we should take?*
>
> Alex: *I think you should follow those teenagers, but don't rule out other possibilities yet.*
>
> Kate: *We haven't.*
>
> Alex: *Notice everything. Does anyone have anything to gain by forcing this riverboat company out of business? Who owns the company? Do any company leaders have any enemies?*

Kate moved to the side, and Elizabeth typed:
> *Those are good questions. I think we have enough to get us started now. Thanks.*

Alex: *This will be tough. Send me the names of the riverboat companies, and I'll do some background research.*

Elizabeth: *Will do. We'll get started now. Talk to you soon!*

Just then, there was a knock on the door, and the two girls peeked out of their doorway into the living area. It was Uncle Dan. "I hope I didn't wake you all up," he said.

Robert Anderson invited his brother in. "No, we're still wide awake. Come on in."

Uncle Dan wheeled into the room. He looked worried. "My friend Lyndel needs me to go with him to the police station. He owns River City Cruises—the one with all the boats breaking down. Now, one of his boats has been spray-painted by vandals. Neon pink! Of all people for this to happen to. He's got enough to deal with already."

"I'm so sorry," said Sue Anderson. "What is this world coming to?"

Mr. Anderson rubbed his chin. "Lyndel. . .I believe that was the name of the captain I helped this morning. Can I do anything?"

Uncle Dan shook his head. "No. He just wants me to come for moral support. I wanted to let you know I'll be gone for a while, but you can reach me on my cell phone."

He said good night and left.

The two girls looked at each other, and retreated into their room. Vandals! Could the two events be related?

Teenagers Ahead!

The next morning, Kate, Elizabeth, and Biscuit stopped by the breakfast buffet at the hotel on their way to the Little Church at La Villita. Kate finished off a banana, an orange, a chocolate chip muffin, and was working on a cherry Danish.

"I don't know where you put it all," said Elizabeth, laughing. "You're like a hummingbird—so tiny, yet always eating."

Kate smiled and kept working on her last bites. "I can't help it. I'm always starving," she said. "But then, last month I went about two weeks when I wasn't hungry at all. I hardly ate a thing, and my mom thought I was sick. Go figure."

When the girls arrived at the church, Gary smiled and welcomed the girls. "I'm so glad you're here. Elizabeth, Kate told me you are musical. The girl who was planning to lead music for us lost her voice. Would you mind leading the children in a few songs, while we finish setting up?"

Elizabeth looked at the children gathering in front of the church. The Bible club wasn't supposed to start for another half hour, but these children looked eager to begin.

"No problem," Elizabeth told the man, and walked up

the steps in front of the small church.

"Good morning, everyone! My name is Elizabeth. Welcome to Bible Camp!"

A dozen pairs of eyes looked at her in expectation. "How many of you like to sing?"

A few of the children raised their hands. "Great!" Elizabeth told them. "Why don't you, and you, and you come up here and help me lead everyone in some songs?"

She pointed out three of the children who'd raised their hands, and they scrambled up the steps to stand next to her.

Elizabeth tried to think of songs everyone would know. "Let's sing, 'This Little Light of Mine,' " she said, and started singing.

Only a few of them seemed to know the song, but they were quick learners. The group continued with "Jesus Loves Me," and Elizabeth taught them the motions to some silly songs. The crowd grew as more children joined the group. Before long, Gary signaled to Elizabeth that she could stop, and the man climbed the steps and addressed the group.

"Welcome to Bible Camp!" the man said. "We're glad you're here today. We're going to have a lot of fun."

As Gary continued telling the children about the upcoming games, snacks, and Bible stories, Elizabeth heard snickering. She turned to see the same group of teenagers from the day before. They were standing in the shadows of a small art museum, and they seemed to be making fun of Gary.

Why, the nerve! she thought. *Well, good. You're here, right under my nose. And I'll find a way to make you 'fess up!*

Gary didn't miss a beat, though. "Hey guys! Glad you're here. Come on up here with the rest of us. We'll put you to work!" Gary's smile was genuine, and the teenagers looked embarrassed.

"No thanks," said Red-cap Boy, and the group shuffled away.

"Come back if you change your minds," called Gary, and continued his speech.

The group of forty children was divided into three rotating groups: games, crafts, and Bible stories. Kate was helping with crafts, and moved to a long table set against the side of the old church. Elizabeth moved inside the church to help keep the children quiet during the Bible story time.

As she was about to enter the tall double doors, she noticed a movement to her right, in the shadows.

Those pesky teenagers again! Why won't they just leave us alone? Leaning over the railing, she peered further into the shadows, and saw a little girl. *Is that the little girl we saw with her mother on the Riverwalk yesterday?*

Biscuit, whose leash was attached to the railing, barked and wagged his tail.

"Hello?" Elizabeth called. "Would you like to join us? We're going to have a lot of fun!"

Silence.

Elizabeth moved down the steps, unhooked Biscuit's leash from the railing, and stepped into the shadows where the girl was hiding.

"What is your name?" she asked.

No response.

"Would you like to pet Biscuit? He seems to like you," she told the little girl.

Slowly, the girl lifted her eyes just enough to look at Biscuit. Her hair covered most of her face, and she reached out a tiny hand and rubbed Biscuit behind the ears. His tail wagged even more, but he remained calm. It was almost as if he knew he needed to be gentle with this girl.

"Why don't you come inside with me?" Elizabeth asked, and took the girl by the hand. The girl looked only at the ground, and her thick, dark curls cascaded around her face. But when Elizabeth led her up the steps and into the church, she didn't resist.

The two girls, with Biscuit, found seats behind the others. A brunette girl from Kate's church was just starting. "Hello, everyone. My name is Charis, and I'm going to tell you a story."

Elizabeth was thrilled when the girl began placing felt figures on a flannel board. Looking around the room, she saw every child's eyes glued to the board.

The little girl beside her kept her head down, with her hair covering her face. But those two large brown eyes peered upward, taking in every word of the story. Elizabeth started to gently push the girl's hair away from her eyes, but the girl moved out of reach.

"I'm sorry," Elizabeth whispered, and turned her attention back to the story of Jonah. *I wonder what makes her so afraid of people.*

Eventually, Charis finished the story and asked everyone to bow for prayer. During the prayer, Elizabeth heard rustling beside her, but figured it was just Biscuit. When she opened her eyes, the little girl was gone.

The rest of the morning passed quickly, and before long, Kate approached Elizabeth outside the church. Her hands were covered in marker and glue.

"I don't know why Gary asked me to help with crafts. It was fun, but I'm not very crafty. Give me some nuts and bolts and wires, and I'm good to go. But ask me to glue a circle onto a piece of paper, and I'm all thumbs. It was fun, though," said Kate, using the back of her hand to push her glasses up on her nose. She pulled her backpack onto her shoulders, getting ready to leave.

"Did you see a little girl leave the church? She had thick, dark curls, and she walked with her head down," Elizabeth asked her.

Charis approached them, hearing the last part of the conversation. "I noticed she left early. What happened? She listened to every word I said, but after the prayer, she was gone!"

Kate nodded. "I did see her leave, but I was covered in

glue at the moment."

Biscuit barked and wagged his tail. "I'll bet Biscuit can find her, if she's still around here," Elizabeth said.

Kate knelt down and stroked the little dog's fur. "Can you find the little girl, Biscuit? Take us to her!"

With a bark that told of understanding, the dog led the way. Kate held his leash, and Elizabeth waved to Charis before following Kate and Biscuit.

In and out of old stucco buildings Biscuit led them, stopping here and there, sniffing an area before moving forward. Suddenly, his ears perked up, his tail stuck straight out, and he growled.

Pulling the leash tight, he moved forward, practically dragging Kate. "Whoa, boy! Where are you taking us?"

Biscuit continued pursuing some unknown party, Kate and Elizabeth in his wake. They rounded the corner of an old building just in time to see a flash of red ball cap disappear behind another building.

Elizabeth and Kate looked at each other, but Biscuit gave no time for the girls to talk. Tugging fiercely on his leash, he pulled Kate, with Elizabeth following.

Before long, they had left the vicinity of the Riverwalk. "I sure hope Biscuit can lead us back, because I'm lost!" said Elizabeth. Then, she saw a sign that read THE ALAMO, with an arrow pointing to the right.

Biscuit barked and pulled even harder at his leash.

"Come on," said Kate, and they let Biscuit lead the way.

They kept seeing glimpses of the red hat ahead and knew they were following the group of teenagers.

Before long, they arrived at the Alamo site. It was crowded with tourists, and the girls could no longer see the gang of teens.

"Whoa," breathed Kate. "So this is really the Alamo. I've always wanted to see the place where the Texans won their famous battle."

Elizabeth stopped in her tracks. "Kate," she said. "We lost the Alamo."

Kate stopped abruptly. "What? That can't be true. In all the old Westerns, the cowboys ride around saying, 'Remember the Alamo!' Why would they want to remember it if they lost?"

Elizabeth took Kate by the arm and led her toward the old structure, which was now a museum.

"Come on, Yank. You've got some thangs to larn," Elizabeth said in an exaggerated Texas accent.

"Yank? Who are you calling a Yank? Exactly what is a Yank, anyway?" Kate asked.

Elizabeth laughed. "A Yankee is just a person from up north who doesn't really understand the Southern way of life."

"Well, technically, Texas isn't in the South. It's in the West," Kate corrected her.

"The Southwest," Elizabeth answered playfully. "Actually, we're not Southern or Western. We're just plain Texan."

They stopped just outside the large wooden doors and read a small plaque on the wall. "Originally named Misión San Antonio de Valero, the Alamo served as home to missionaries and their Indian converts for nearly seventy years."

"Mission? The Alamo was a church?"

"Not exactly. It was a missionary home," Elizabeth clarified. "But it was probably used for church services, too."

"And they blew it up?" Kate asked with disbelief. "Churches are supposed to be safe places!"

Elizabeth took her friend by the arm and led her inside, but not before picking up Biscuit and placing him in her friend's backpack. "Come on. I think it's time for a history lesson."

The girls entered the mission just in time to join a tour group. Kate looked in awe at cannons, rusty pistols, even weathered sticks of dynamite as the tour guide gave them an overview of Texas history.

They were about halfway through the tour when Elizabeth spotted the red cap in the group in front of them. "Look!" she whispered, but Kate ignored her. She was fascinated with the tour guide's words.

Kate raised her hand to ask a question. "So Santa Anna was trying to reclaim Texas to be a part of Mexico?"

"That's correct," the tour guide answered.

Elizabeth tried to get Kate's attention again, but couldn't. The red hat was moving toward the exit.

"And Santa Anna's men lost the first and second tries,

but came back a third time and climbed the walls?" Kate continued.

"Yes," the woman answered. "Many more of Santa Anna's men were killed than Texans. But there were more to start with so when all was said and done, Santa Anna and his men won the victory."

"It doesn't seem like a fair fight to me," Kate said.

"Many Texans felt that way. That's why the battle at the Alamo caused many to join Sam Houston's army, which resulted in Santa Anna's defeat," the woman said.

"Now I get it. That's why they wanted to remember the Alamo. They didn't want to let Santa Anna bully them anymore," Kate said.

The boy with the red hat, along with the rest of his gang, were leaving the building. Elizabeth grabbed Kate by the arm and said, "It's been a wonderful tour. Thank you so much. We're sorry we have to leave now."

"Hey! What are you—" For the first time, Kate caught a glimpse of the gang of teenagers just as the door was closing.

"Oh! Bye!" Kate waved at the group of tourists and followed Elizabeth.

The girls stepped into the bright Texas sunlight and looked around. Nothing. The group had vanished.

Elizabeth shook her head. "I'm glad you're so interested in Texas history, Kate. Really, I am. But your timing is a little. . .off!"

"Sorry," said Kate. "It's just that I had no idea! I can't

believe I'm really standing at the Alamo! I could be standing in the exact spot where. . .where. . .where John Wayne stood!"

Elizabeth, who had begun moving forward, stopped in her tracks. "Now that sounds exactly like something Alexis would say. You do know John Wayne was an actor in a movie, don't you? He wasn't really at the battle of the Alamo."

Kate giggled. "I know. I just wanted to see what you'd say!"

Biscuit, whose face was poking out of Kate's backpack, became agitated. He began wiggling and barking. Elizabeth reached over, removed Biscuit, and placed him on the ground. She was about to snap his leash into place when the little dog took off running!

"Biscuit, wait!" called Elizabeth, but Biscuit kept running. The girls had no choice but to chase their four-legged sidekick. He didn't make it easy for them. He dodged in and out of tourists' legs, causing several to drop their bags. Kate and Elizabeth followed after him at high speed, calling out, "Excuse me!" and "So sorry!"

At last, Biscuit stopped. When they caught up with him, he was barking fiercely at the gang of teenagers, and had Mr. Red-cap backed into a corner.

"Whoa, boy! What is your problem? Why don't you like me, little dog?" the boy was saying. His back was flat against the brick wall of an art shop, and the customers and other tourists were gathering.

53

"Biscuit! Stop that!" said Kate, kneeling beside him and attaching his leash. "Sorry about that," she said to the boy. "I don't know what's gotten into him."

Biscuit continued growling, but submitted to Kate.

The boy, who looked to be fifteen or sixteen, said, "This has never happened before. Dogs usually love me. I have two dogs at home."

Elizabeth spoke up. "Maybe he smells your other dogs and doesn't like them."

The boy laughed. "I doubt it. My mom can't stand the smell of dogs. She bathes them in some kind of girly lavender wash twice a week."

Kate's jaw dropped. "Lavender? Your mom bathes your dogs in lavender? Biscuit hates lavender!"

The group took a moment to process that, then they all burst into laughter.

"Mystery solved!" the boy said.

"At least one of them, anyway," said Elizabeth.

Red-cap Boy looked at her strangely, then held out his hand. "I'm José. My friends call me Joe. This is Maria and Pedro." He indicated his friends.

Elizabeth shook each of their hands, and said, "Nice to meet you. I'm Elizabeth, and this is Kate. And the growling, four-legged fellow is Biscuit."

Joe knelt down and spoke softly to Biscuit in Spanish. Ever so slowly, he reached out his hand and gently touched the dog's coat.

Gradually, Biscuit relaxed. He never wagged his tail or licked the boy's hand as he usually did when someone was kind to him. His look seemed to say, "I guess I won't attack you. But I'm not going to be your friend, either."

"Well, I guess that's a start. So what other mystery were you trying to solve, Elizabeth?" Joe asked, looking down at her with a crooked smile.

Elizabeth blushed. *Why am I blushing?* She stole a quick glance at Kate, who leveled her with a steely stare.

"Oh, she was just talking about the mysteries of life," Kate rescued her. "That's Elizabeth. The philosopher. She's always pondering the deep mysteries of the universe, and stuff like that."

Joe looked at Kate, then back at Elizabeth. "That's, uh. . . nice," he said.

Elizabeth blushed even more, then said, "Well, we'd better be going. We'll see you around!"

Chased!

The group waved good-bye, and the girls headed toward the Riverwalk, Biscuit on his leash. "What was that about?" Kate asked.

"What do you mean?" Elizabeth asked, trying to play dumb.

"I mean that little googly-eyed Romeo and Juliet scene back there. Don't forget, Miss Anderson, that Señor Charming is one of our prime suspects."

"I don't know what you're talking about," said Elizabeth.

Kate gave her a hard stare, but said nothing.

Finally Elizabeth said, "Okay. He has a nice smile. His teeth are so white, and those dimples. . .never mind. But I was *not* googly-eyed."

Kate rolled her eyes. "The lady doth protest too much, methinks," she said.

"Huh?" Elizabeth looked at her friend as if she were speaking a foreign language.

"It's from Shakespeare's *Hamlet*. It means that by denying so strongly that you were googly-eyed, it actually proves my point that you were googly-eyed."

Elizabeth laughed. "Kate, you are truly one of a kind."

Kate smiled.

"And I was *not* googly-eyed. Whatever that means," Elizabeth said.

"My point exactly." Kate gave a smug grin.

Elizabeth changed the subject. "Look, there's a riverboat getting ready to leave. Let's ride!"

"I don't know. After what's been happening with these boats, I'm not sure I want to take the chance."

"Aww, come on. It's part of the San Antonio experience. Besides, maybe we'll get some more clues," Elizabeth encouraged.

Kate adjusted her glasses. "Santa Anna Tours," she read the side of the boat. "The company that crashed into the stage last night was River City Cruises. I guess this one's safe."

"Santa Anna Tours. . . ," Elizabeth read. "That must be a new company. River City is the only one I've ever ridden." She started to get in line, but Kate grabbed her arm.

"Wait. I need to clean my glasses," she said, and Elizabeth followed her to a nearby water fountain. When they returned to the line, they were surprised to see Joe and his friends already sitting on the boat.

"Hola, chicas," he said with his dimpled grin. "Going for a ride?"

Elizabeth suddenly felt shy. She looked to Kate for a signal of what to do.

"You bet we're gonna ride," Kate told him, giving him her fiercest stare. Moving onto the platform, she held his gaze, and forgot to look where she was stepping.

"Watch out, miss!" cried the captain, but it was too late. Kate made a loud splash as she fell into the water.

Biscuit followed with a smaller splash. The little dog frantically paddled to the edge of the Riverwalk and climbed out, but Kate looked like she was drowning.

"Help!" she cried between sputters. "Help! I can't swim! Somebody help me!" She splashed and flailed. Elizabeth read the terror in her friend's face.

"Kate! Stand up! The water is only waist deep!" Elizabeth called out, but Kate was too terrified to understand.

Suddenly, there was another loud splash.

Joe!

The boy grabbed Kate and hoisted the tiny, dripping girl into his arms. "Calm down. I've got you," he said.

Kate clung to the boy for dear life. He walked her to the edge and set her on the concrete walkway.

Another tourist, a woman with two children, pulled a beach towel out of her tote bag and draped it around Kate's shoulders. "Here you go, honey. You'll be just fine."

Kate nodded her thanks as Joe fished around in the water for Kate's glasses. He handed them to her and grinned. Looking at Elizabeth, he said, "Good thing I was here to save your friend. I guess that makes me a hero."

Elizabeth busied herself, using the towel to dry Kate's

Elizabeth's SAN ANTONIO SLEUTHING

hair and clothes. "Are you okay?" she asked her friend.

"Physically, I'm fine," Kate said. "My ego, on the other hand, is suffering."

Elizabeth laughed. "I suppose I'll have to give you swimming lessons when we get back to the hotel."

"No thanks. I'd prefer to stay inside with my computers and books and gadgets. It's safer that way," she said.

The captain, a short, bald man with a protruding belly, had been useless during this ordeal. Laughing nervously, he said, "Okay, folks. The excitement's over. Now who wants to go for a ride?"

Elizabeth was surprised when Kate walked to the small boarding platform. "You still want to ride?" she asked.

Kate leaned close and whispered, "Of course I want to ride. We have a mystery to solve, don't we?"

Elizabeth chuckled and followed her friend onto the boat. They sat on the opposite side of the boat from the three teenagers. Joe, now soaked, sat directly across from Elizabeth. He flashed her that grin, and she determined then and there to not look at him again.

As the boat purred to a start, the captain picked up his microphone. "Welcome, ladies and gentlemen, to Santa Anna Tours. We are thrilled to have you as passengers, and we believe you'll find our Riverwalk tour superior, in every way, to our competitor's tour. Please remain seated at all times, and keep your arms and legs inside."

"Eeeeeeeeeeeek!" screamed a middle-aged woman

sitting in the middle section of the boat. "A snake! There's a snake in the boat!"

Her husband leaned over and picked up a deadly looking rubber snake. "Calm down, Rita. It isn't real."

Rita covered her mouth with her hand and took a deep breath. "Well, it certainly looked real," she said.

The captain leaned over and took the snake from the man.

"I'm so sorry. I don't know how this could have happened." He eyed Joe, but the boy just returned the captain's gaze with an angelic look.

"I'll bet you a chimichanga I know who put that snake there," Kate whispered as the boat continued on its way. The captain pointed out all the familiar sights, explaining how the Riverwalk had been built for the 1968 World's Fair. Elizabeth never grew tired of hearing how their hotel—the Palacio del Rio—had been assembled and furnished elsewhere, and put in place—room by room—by a huge crane, as builders scrambled to get things ready for the World's Fair. They were able to get the hotel put together just in time.

"Stay calm, folks. We're gonna get you out of this. Please stay in the boat," they heard a man's voice over a microphone up ahead of them. The Santa Anna passengers strained to see what the commotion was about.

Up ahead was a River City Cruise boat filled with passengers. And it seemed to be filling with water. The captain was trying to keep the passengers calm and steer the boat to the side of the river.

The Santa Anna captain said nothing. Did nothing. Just kept on with his tour script.

"Uh, excuse me, sir?" Elizabeth raised her hand.

"Yes, miss? Did you have a question?" the captain acknowledged her with a artificial smile.

"Don't you think we should stop and try to help those people?" she asked.

The man laughed and said, "Oh, they'll be fine. Things like that happen all the time to River City Cruises. You all made the right choice, choosing Santa Anna Tours! Of course, if you're in the mood for a swim, perhaps you should try River City next time. They'll be sure to deliver!" The captain laughed a little too loudly, and the crowd responded with a few chuckles. No one seemed to think his joke was very funny.

Once again, Elizabeth heard a loud splash—and another. Joe and Pedro had jumped in the water and were wading to the stranded boat. The Santa Anna boat continued, with the captain desperately trying to regain his audience's attention.

"Well, well, this has certainly been an exciting ride today, hasn't it, folks? Let me direct your attention to the bridge up ahead. That was the first bridge built here on the Riverwalk. . . ."

As the captain droned on, Elizabeth watched the two boys push the stranded boat to the edge. Then they helped the passengers onto the sidewalk.

"I can't figure them out," she whispered to Kate. "They are our main suspects in. . .several mysteries. But they seem to be pretty good guys."

Kate said, "Yep, this is a job for the Camp Club Girls."

Elizabeth's gaze left the boys for a moment and landed on Maria, sitting by herself. She, too, was watching the scene behind her. "You're right," she whispered. "But first, I think we need to interview someone."

When the boat ride was over, Kate handed the towel back to the kind lady. "Thank you," she said.

"No problem, honey. I'm just glad you're okay," the lady said.

The two girls waited for Maria to disembark, and the girl smiled at them. "That was some boat ride!" she told them.

"I'll say," answered Kate.

The girl smiled, and the three stood in awkward silence. "Well, I guess I'd better go look for my cousins," she said.

"Your cousins?" Elizabeth and Kate exclaimed.

"Yeah," she said. "Sometimes I'm not proud of that fact. Other times, like just now, I remember that they're pretty good guys."

"Do you mind if we walk with you?" asked Elizabeth.

"Sure!" the girl said. "I mean, no, I don't mind."

All around them, bright streamers of *papel picado*— hand-cut paper decorations—seemed to dance to the mariachi music playing in the distance, and the girls naturally walked in time with the rhythm.

"What makes you say that sometimes you're not proud to be related to them?" asked Kate.

"Oh, you know how boys can be," she said.

Elizabeth and Kate nodded.

"And my cousins—Joe, especially—is all boy. He loves to get into mischief, play pranks. Sometimes I wonder why I hang out with them so much," she said. "But they are pretty fun, and it beats staying at home, watching television."

"So you live around here?" Elizabeth asked.

"Yeah, we live a couple of blocks from here. Our parents work near here, and it makes it nice. We don't need a car. We can walk or ride our scooters everywhere we need to go."

"What kinds of pranks do they pull?" pressed Elizabeth. She was determined to wrangle a confession out of someone.

"Oh, you know," the girl said. "This and that." She was beginning to look uncomfortable. Just then, they rounded a curve in the Riverwalk and saw the boys ahead. They were standing at attention, hands by their sides, as a police officer spoke with the captain of the River City Cruise boat—the boat they'd helped rescue.

As the girls drew closer, they could hear the agitated voice of the captain saying, "It's sabotage, I'm telling you. Someone has been meddling with my boats. And these boys seem to be hanging around the Riverwalk with too much time on their hands."

The police officer looked at the boys. "What have you been doing all morning?"

Joe spoke with respect. "We attended some kind of Bible club this morning, down at the church at La Villita. Then we went to the Alamo. After that, we came back here to ride on that other riverboat. We just jumped in to help him because he was stranded. No one else helped him, so we did."

The captain spoke up. "These boys are always hanging around whenever something bad happens. I can't prove it, but I think they're behind the problems I'm having with my boats."

The officer wrote on a notepad, and then questioned the boys further. "You say you were at a Bible club, then the Alamo before you rode on the other boat?"

"Yes, sir," Joe answered.

"Can you prove that?" the officer asked him. "Did anyone else see you at those places?"

Elizabeth stepped forward then. "Excuse me, sir, but these boys are telling the truth. I saw them at those places."

"And your name is. . . ?" questioned the police officer.

"Elizabeth Anderson," she replied.

"And I'm Kate Oliver," Kate spoke up. "I saw them, too. Elizabeth and I are helping with the Bible club. I can take you to my youth minister, if you'd like, and he'll verify that."

The police officer eyed the girls, then shut his notepad. "That won't be necessary." He looked at the boat's captain.

"I know you're frustrated. And it does appear that someone is trying to sabotage your business. But without proof, I can't hold these boys. It looks to me like they were just doing a good deed."

The captain looked sheepish. He took off his hat and nervously twisted it in his hands. "I'm sorry, boys. I guess I jumped to conclusions. I'm just anxious to get to the bottom of all these mishaps. I do appreciate your help today."

Joe smiled. "That's okay, sir. I hope everything works out for you, and you catch the real bad guys."

The police officer dismissed the boys and continued talking to the captain. Joe and Pedro sighed with relief and turned to Elizabeth and Kate.

"Thanks," the boys told them.

"I don't know what would have happened if you two hadn't shown up," said Pedro.

"Yeah. I was afraid we were going to end up in hand-cuffs or something, all for trying to help the guy," Joe added.

Marie looked smugly at her cousins. "I told you all to quit playing all those tricks. People can tell when you're up to no good, and then you get blamed for worse things. It's your own fault."

Elizabeth couldn't resist cutting into the conversation. "And exactly what tricks are you talking about, Maria?"

Joe laughed nervously. "Oh, Maria is *loco*. Crazy. She doesn't know what she's talking about. Just ignore her."

"Would any of those tricks happen to involve a water

balloon?" Elizabeth pressed. It didn't matter to her whether or not these boys were criminals or just pranksters. She knew they were guilty of something, and she was going to get to the bottom of this.

Joe smiled a cat-ate-the-canary smile and said nothing. Pedro laughed, and Maria just shook her head before launching into a tirade of rapidly spoken Spanish words. Elizabeth caught a word here and there, but she didn't know very much Spanish.

Something in the shadows caught her eye. Was that the captain of the Santa Anna? And the man he was talking to looked familiar. . . .

It's the rude man from the boat yesterday! The one who was complaining about the River City boats right after the boat died! And. . .what was that on his hands?

She nudged Kate and pointed. Maria continued on with her tirade as the boys tried to ignore their cousin. Joe, noticing that Elizabeth's and Kate's attention was elsewhere, followed their gaze.

The captain of the Santa Anna boat pulled a wad of money out of his pocket and handed it to the man, who stuffed it in his own pocket with fingers stained with neon pink paint. Too late, the men noticed they had an audience.

"Hey! What are you kids doing?" the captain yelled.

Each member of the group seemed to know, without being told, that they had just witnessed something sinister. They took off running. Biscuit, who'd been comfortably napping in Kate's backpack after his morning swim, suddenly came to life. Barking and growling, the little dog wiggled his way out of the backpack, scattering a stack of Kate's business cards in the process.

"Biscuit!" Kate yelled, and scooped her dog into her arms before the men reached him.

"This way!" called Joe, and motioned for them to enter a doorway to. . .Elizabeth had no idea where the doorway led. But she and Kate followed. Joe slammed the door behind them, and Elizabeth peered out the small window.

The two men had stopped running. The captain bent and retrieved one of Kate's cards. He read it, looked toward the doorway, and slipped the card into his pocket.

As the pink-handed man walked toward the doorway, Joe called out, "Get down!" The boy clicked the dead bolt on the door just before they heard the door being pulled. The man on the other side of the door began rattling, and then his shadow blocked the light coming through the window as he peered inside.

Elizabeth's heart pounded. Who were those men? And what were they doing? Why was the captain paying the other man?

Deep voices came from the other side of the door. "It's locked. Do you want me to go after them?" Elizabeth recognized the voice of the taller man with painted hands.

"Leave 'em alone for now. I have an idea that will shut them up, once and for all."

The Quiet Child

The five young people looked at each other and sighed in unison.

"What was that about?" asked Maria.

"Those guys aren't up to any good, that's for sure," said Joe.

Elizabeth stood on her tiptoes and peered out the tiny window. The men were gone. "Kate. . .we need to get back to the hotel," she said.

"I know! My clothes are still wet, and my sneakers are sloshing," Kate complained.

"And you need to check your blog," Elizabeth added.

"Check my blog? That's right. I need to update my blog," she replied.

"Kate, those men have your card," Elizabeth told her.

Kate's eyes grew wide and round. "My business cards! That's right, they scattered when Biscuit tried to escape. . . ."

"Well, as long as we are careful, it could be a good thing. Maybe we can figure out a way to mislead them or something," Elizabeth told her.

Joe spoke up then. "A blog? What kind of blog? And you have a business card? How old are you, anyway?"

Kate adjusted her glasses then addressed the group. "I know this may come as a surprise to you, but Elizabeth and I are detectives."

The group burst into laughter, including Elizabeth. Kate sounded so serious.

"Laugh if you want to, but it's the truth. And I have a blog you can access online. I discuss different mysteries and ways to solve them."

"Whoa," said Pedro. "We don't know anything about the Internet."

"Yes, we do!" said Maria. "Remember, we had to take that class in school?"

"Oh yeah. A lot of the kids at school have computers at home, but none of us do. So we're pretty clueless when it comes to that type of stuff," said Joe.

"A lot of people don't have computers at home. But I'm sure your library has a computer you can use for free," Elizabeth said.

Joe smiled at her again, and she looked away.

Stop looking at him. Look at Maria when you talk, Elizabeth told herself.

"And if I went to the library, who would teach me how to use the computer?" he asked.

"The librarian," said Kate. "By the way, can somebody please tell me where we are?"

"We're in a secret passageway. I thought you detectives would know all about that," Joe teased.

"Well, you obviously knew it was here. I'm hoping you also know where it leads!" Kate retorted.

"Follow me," Maria chimed in. She began walking down the long hallway, and the others followed her. They turned to the right, and then pushed open some swinging doors that led into a kitchen. Immediately, people called out greetings in Spanish. Elizabeth recognized the logo on the red aprons.

This is the kitchen of Rio Rio!

One woman began speaking in rapid-fire Spanish to Joe. She was standing over a dish of the most delicious-looking tamales Elizabeth had ever seen.

Those tamales! Those are the tamales I love so much!

Joe turned to Elizabeth and Kate. "I'd like you to meet my mama, Elena Garcia. Mama, this is Kate," he gestured, and the woman smiled.

"And *this*," he said with emphasis, "is *Elizabeth*."

The woman lifted her eyebrows at her son, then smiled at Elizabeth, who could feel herself turning every shade of red. *Why did he say it like that?*

"It's very nice to meet both of you," the woman said. Then, she looked at Elizabeth. "Don't you let Jose give you a hard time. He is. . .how you say? . . . All bark and no bite."

Now it was Joe's turn to blush, and the group laughed.

Biscuit chose that moment to bark, and several people in the kitchen turned to look at the little dog. Joe's mother began speaking in rapid Spanish once again, finishing with, "*Andale! Andale!*"

Elizabeth knew she was telling them to hurry and get out. Dogs weren't allowed in restaurant kitchens.

Kate scooped Biscuit into her arms and said, "We need to be going. Thanks for everything," and looked for an exit sign.

"It was very nice to meet you, Mrs. Garcia," Elizabeth told the woman, and followed Kate through a door.

Once inside the door, they realized they were in a supply closet.

"Well, this is a little embarrassing," said Kate, turning to go back through the door.

As the girls re-entered the kitchen, the staff clapped and laughed. Joe stepped forward and said, "Allow me to accompany you," in a gallant tone.

Red-faced, the two girls followed their guide through another door, down a short hallway, and finally stepped into the sunlight of the Riverwalk.

"Thanks, Joe. We'll. . .see ya around," Kate told him, and began moving toward the hotel.

"Yeah, thanks," called Elizabeth with a slight wave. Joe watched them until they were out of sight.

●—●—●

An hour later, the girls lay across their beds in the hotel room talking on their cell phones and munching on French fries. Kate had set her phone for a conference call, and amazingly, had gotten in touch with each of the other Camp Club Girls.

"Okay," said Sydney. "Let me get this straight. Elizabeth got hit by a water balloon while riding in a River City Cruise boat, and another lady found a rubber snake at her feet while riding a Santa Anna boat. River City keeps having mechanical problems, but you don't think the mechanical problems are related to the pranks."

"We did to begin with," said Kate. "But we're pretty sure we know who the pranksters are, and they seem pretty harmless. I told you about the two men who chased us. And the tall, skinny guy had pink hands—the color one of the River City boats was painted. I think those men are responsible for the vandalism. At least, Elizabeth *hopes* it's those men."

"What is that supposed to mean?" asked Elizabeth.

"You know exactly what it means," said Kate in a teasing voice. "Elizabeth is swooning over one of the pranksters."

"I am not!" said Elizabeth, and the other girls began asking questions, all at once.

"Tell us more, Kate! Who is this guy? What is his name?" they asked.

Elizabeth pulled the pillow over her head, but continued listening to the conversation.

"His name is José Garcia," Kate said with a dramatic accent.

"Ooh! Is he from Mexico? I could be related to him!" said Alex. "If you marry him, Elizabeth, we could end up being cousins!"

"Y'all, stop it! I'm not marrying anybody. Kate is just making stuff up," Elizabeth defended herself, throwing a pillow at her roommate. "And he likes to be called Joe."

"Hmmmmm. . .Elizabeth Garcia," teased Bailey. "It has a ring to it."

The other girls laughed, until finally McKenzie said, "You guys, leave Elizabeth alone."

"Thank you, Mac," said Elizabeth.

"I'm sure she'll invite us all to the wedding, when the time comes," McKenzie continued.

"*Mac!*" Elizabeth yelled into the phone, and everyone laughed again.

"All right, already," Kate said. "Sorry I brought it up, Elizabeth. I just couldn't resist. Now, can we please get back to the matter at hand? What should be our next step in solving this mystery?"

"Tell us more about the two men," Sydney said.

"Well, the captain is shorter, bald, pudgy. . .and he wears a captain's hat," Elizabeth responded.

"Like the hat the captain wore on *Gilligan's Island*?" Alex asked.

"Oh, I've seen that show! That's an old one. And yes, the hat is exactly like that," Elizabeth said. "And the other guy is tall and skinny, and seems to take orders from the captain."

"It sounds to me like you need to focus your investigation on Gilligan and the Skipper," said Bailey. Once again, she had come up with the perfect nicknames for their suspects.

73

Alex spoke up again. "Kate, you took your bag of gadgets along, didn't you?"

"Do you even have to ask?" Kate responded.

"Did you bring along one of those little listening thing-a-ma-jiggers?" Alex continued.

"You mean a bug?" Kate asked.

"Yeah," Alex laughed. "A bug. But 'thing-a-ma-jigger' is so much more fun to say."

Everyone laughed, and Bailey spoke up. "How far away can you be, and still hear a conversation through the bug?"

"That shouldn't be a problem," said Kate. "There are plenty of hiding places."

"But where will you plant the bug?" asked McKenzie. "Those men sound scary. I don't want you to do anything dangerous."

"We'll be careful," Elizabeth assured her. "There are several boarding areas for the boats, and they're often left unmanned when the boat is on a tour. We can probably put a bug on the fence railing at one of those areas."

"Yeah, and then we can hang out at one of the nearby restaurants eating chips and salsa until something happens," Kate said.

The other girls laughed. "Always thinking about food," said Sydney.

"Hey, if we're going to sit and wait, we might as well do something constructive," Kate retorted.

The girls laughed, and Elizabeth spoke up again. "Our

biggest problem is that the two men know who we are. Kate dropped a business card, and one of them picked it up. Now they know we're sleuths."

Alex said, "Hey, maybe you could use that to your advantage. They know you are just kids, and they probably won't expect much of you. I remember an episode of *Hawaii Five-O* where McGarrett went undercover as a convict, and made it look like the police were after him. Maybe you can pretend to focus in on someone else as the guilty party, and the men will leave you alone."

"Hey, that might work," said Kate. "We could ask Joe to be our undercover guy, and act guilty. . . ."

Alex laughed. "Joe, huh? Well, that would be appropriate."

"What do you mean?" asked Elizabeth.

"The episode I'm thinking of was titled, 'The Ways of Love.' "

Everyone laughed, and Elizabeth said, "I'm never speaking to any of you again. For five whole minutes, anyway. Good-bye." She clicked her phone shut and pulled the pillow over her head again. The other girls recognized the teasing in Elizabeth's voice and laughed.

Kate finally hung up. "Hey, you're not really mad, are you?" she asked.

"No," Elizabeth said. "But I'm not googly-eyed, and I didn't swoon."

Kate ignored her friend's last comment, and instead opened up her laptop. "Now, to update my blog," she said.

Elizabeth watched her log into her stats page. Sure enough, comments waited. Clicking on the first of two, she read, *"Back off. You're in over your head!"*

The next read, *"You leave us alone, and we'll leave your little dog alone."*

The two girls stared at the screen.

"Elizabeth, those guys are serious. They threatened Biscuit! What are we going to do?"

Elizabeth stared at the screen, forming a silent prayer. Water balloons and rubber snakes were one thing. Threatening Biscuit was an entirely different matter. *What should we do, Lord?*

A Bible verse popped into her head, one of the first verses she had learned as a small child. She had actually learned it as a song. Elizabeth took a deep breath and began singing the words to Psalm 56:3. "When I am afraid, I will trust in You, I will trust in You, I will trust in You. When I am afraid I will trust in You, when I am afraid."

Kate leaned back on the bed and looked at the ceiling. "I know we're supposed to trust God in all things. But I also think we're supposed to use wisdom. I don't want to do anything to put Biscuit in danger and just assume God will rescue him."

Elizabeth reread the words on the screen. After a moment, she said, "You're right. We need to be careful, and use wisdom. But we won't let those men ruin our good time. We'll just be extra careful, keep Biscuit close, and trust God to show us what to do."

"Do you think we should let an adult know what's going on?" Kate asked.

Elizabeth leaned back on her elbows. "Probably. And I think I know exactly who to tell. . . ."

●—●—●

Later that evening, Elizabeth and Kate leaned on the counter in the hotel lobby, waiting for Uncle Dan to finish with a customer. He handed the woman a key and said, "Enjoy your stay."

As soon as the woman was out of earshot, he wheeled his chair back to the girls, and said, "Okay, I'm all ears. Tell me again how you got mixed up in all of this."

Elizabeth and Kate took turns filling him in on the details. "At first, I thought Joe and his friends were probably behind the problems with the boats, but I don't think that anymore," Elizabeth told her uncle.

Uncle Dan looked out the glass doors toward the Riverwalk. A Santa Anna boat was puttering by. "Ever since Santa Anna Tours opened for business, River City Cruises has had problems. They've been in business here for decades, and have a spotless record for safety and customer satisfaction. I've wondered about Santa Anna all along."

The girls waited and listened. During Uncle Dan's time in the military, he had worked for military intelligence. If anyone knew how to find clues and solve a mystery, it was him.

Uncle Dan leaned back in his chair and looked at them. "I want you girls to lay low until I've had a chance to think about this. Stay close to the hotel tonight, and keep a close watch on Biscuit. Let's all sleep on it, and we'll talk more tomorrow. I think we may be able to catch these guys, once and for all."

The girls agreed, and left Uncle Dan to his work. Holding Biscuit tightly, Kate said, "Let's go find something to eat."

Just as they turned to leave, Mr. and Mrs. Anderson walked into the lobby, James tagging behind them. "There you are!" said Mrs. Anderson. "We've hardly seen you girls today. Are you hungry?"

The girls nodded. Biscuit jumped out of Kate's arms and began playing with James.

"Why don't you all go ahead and reserve us a table at the café next door. I just need to do something to my hair, and freshen my lipstick," Mrs. Anderson told them.

"You look beautiful, sweetheart," Mr. Anderson told her, and the woman smiled sweetly at her husband.

"Thank you, darling," she said, "but I don't *feel* beautiful. I'll be right behind you." The woman headed for the elevators, and Mr. Anderson shook his head. "Women. I'll never understand them."

The group headed out the lobby doors and found a table at the nearby café. The waitress smiled at Biscuit as she placed their chips and salsa on the table. Suddenly, the little dog barked and leaped from Kate's lap.

"Biscuit!" the girls called out, but it was too late. Biscuit was in hot pursuit of. . .someone.

The girls and James chased the little dog through the outdoor restaurant, dodging tables and customers, working hard to keep the little dog in sight. Finally, they spotted Biscuit ahead, sitting sweetly and licking a little girl's hand.

Elizabeth gasped when she saw who it was. *The little girl from Bible Camp this morning!*

"Hi!" Elizabeth said, kneeling next to the girl. "Do you remember me? We met this morning."

The girl buried her face in her mother's skirt.

"I'm sorry," Elizabeth said to the woman. "I didn't mean to frighten her."

"It's okay," the woman told her. "Annie is very shy. She loves animals, but people make her nervous. You must be from the Bible camp she attended this morning."

"Yes, ma'am. I'm Elizabeth, and this is Kate and James. And this"—she gestured to the dog still looking up at Annie and wagging his tail—"is Biscuit."

"We hope she'll come back tomorrow," said Kate with a smile. "Same time, same place."

The woman looked sadly at her daughter. "I don't know," she said. "Some children can be so cruel."

Elizabeth and Kate looked at each other, confused. *Why would anyone be cruel to such a sweet little girl?*

The Bible Camp Band

Mr. Anderson approached the group. "Everything okay, Elizabeth?" he asked.

"Oh. Hi, Dad. Yes. This little girl was in our Bible camp this morning, and I guess Biscuit recognized her. He seems to like her!" Elizabeth smiled at the little girl, who was peering through her curls.

"Dan Anderson." Elizabeth's dad held his hand out to the woman.

"Teresa Lopez," the woman replied, returning his handshake. "And this is Annie." She gestured to her daughter, who was now squatting, rubbing Biscuit behind the ears. James knelt, too, and spoke softly to the dog and the girl.

Annie turned her head to the side, and for just a moment, her thick curls fell away from her face to reveal a large red birthmark. It covered the entire left side of her face. James didn't seem to notice, but smiled and looked directly into the girl's eyes. "Biscuit really likes you. He likes me, too. He'll be at Bible Camp tomorrow. Are you coming?"

In that moment, Elizabeth wanted to pick her little brother up and hug him.

He is such a great kid! she thought. *Lord, I take back every bad thought I've ever had about my little brother. He is the best little guy in the world!*

Annie's mother noticed, too, and looked at Mr. Anderson. "What a nice boy you have," she whispered. "Annie's birthmark is called a strawberry hemangioma, and many of the children make fun of her. At home, she's outgoing and playful. Unfortunately, she has learned to be afraid of people she doesn't know."

Mr. Anderson nodded. "She's a beautiful little girl, even with the birthmark. Is it possible to have it removed?"

The woman looked close to tears. "Yes, it is possible, but not probable. It's an expensive operation, and I don't have medical insurance. I'm afraid Annie will have to live with her birthmark. At least until she's older."

Mr. Anderson smiled compassionately. Looking at the girls and James, he said, "We'd better head back to the café. Your mother will wonder where we are."

Elizabeth knelt and whispered to Annie, "I hope you'll come back tomorrow. I was lonely after you left today."

Annie looked into Elizabeth's eyes for just a moment. A smile crossed her face, but was gone in an instant.

"I'll bring her," said Mrs. Lopez, "but I can't promise she'll stay."

Elizabeth, her brother and father, and Kate went back

to their table, where they found Mrs. Anderson munching tortilla chips.

"There you are!" she said. "I knew this was your table, because I saw Kate's backpack, so I sat down and started eating. I knew you'd be back. But then, I started wondering what would happen if someone else had a backpack like Kate's, and I was sitting here eating some stranger's chips."

"I see it didn't stop you." Her husband laughed.

"Well, I thought about leaving the chips alone until I knew for sure, but I was too hungry. Where did y'all go?" she asked.

They took turns telling about Biscuit and the little girl, and Mrs. Anderson listened intently. Finally, she said, "I have a cousin who had something like that. Her mother told her it was where an angel kissed her, and she seemed to accept that when she was very young. But as she got older, she became more self-conscious. Some children made fun of her, and made her life miserable."

"Did she ever get it fixed?" Elizabeth asked her mother.

"Yes. There was some organization. . . . I can't think of the name right now. But a charitable group helped finance surgeries like that for children. Perhaps you could do research on it, girls. I know how you like to chase down mysteries and such," she said.

The girls looked at each other, but said nothing. This was just one of the mysteries they were facing. And quite frankly, the other mystery had them a little nervous.

●━●━●

Morning came a little too early for the girls. They had stayed up late talking and doing Internet research. They'd wanted to update Kate's blog, but decided against it. "It's probably better if they think we haven't checked the blog in a few days. Let them think we don't know anything about their threats," Elizabeth had suggested, and Kate grudgingly agreed.

But in spite of their tiredness, the girls and Biscuit were at the appointed place at a quarter to eight, ready to help with Bible Camp. Mrs. Anderson agreed to drop James off at eight o'clock.

"Elizabeth! Glad you're here. Could you lead the kids in songs again?" Gary asked her.

Elizabeth eyed the keyboard set up to one side of the steps. "May I use the keyboard?" she asked.

Gary looked hesitant. "It's borrowed, and I promised the owner I'd take good care of it. . . ."

Kate stepped forward. "Gary, you don't have anything to worry about. When it comes to keyboards, Elizabeth knows her stuff."

Gary lifted his eyebrows then grinned. Moving his arm in a grand, sweeping gesture, he said, "In that case, be my guest."

Elizabeth smiled and moved to the keyboard. She hadn't played one for several days, and she missed the feeling of her fingers on the piano keys. She adjusted the volume then played through a few scales. Finally, she began playing the tune of one of the songs she'd taught the children the day before.

For a few moments, she became absorbed in the keyboard. She pressed a few buttons, and before long, she had added drum rhythms, bells, and even a comical whistling sound. People stopped what they were doing and gathered to listen to her music.

Elizabeth was surprised when she looked up and realized she had an audience. Normally she was self-conscious when she played in front of people. But this was such a relaxed atmosphere, it didn't feel like a recital or a concert. She smiled and spoke into the microphone Gary had placed in front of her.

"Good morning everyone, and welcome to Bible Camp! Do you remember the song I taught you yesterday? Sing it with me now!"

The children gathered at the church steps began singing loudly, and the teenagers and adults joined in. This continued for several songs until Elizabeth looked up and saw Joe smiling at her from the back of the crowd. She immediately missed a note and forgot the words. She finished the song as gracefully as possible, then handed the microphone to Gary and moved to the side of the crowd.

"Thank you, Elizabeth," Gary said. "Isn't she great? Let's all give her a hand!"

The crowd erupted in applause, and Elizabeth turned

beet red. Then, she felt someone crowding against her leg. She looked down to see a mop of familiar curls. Forgetting herself, she hugged the little girl. "Annie! You came!"

The girl smiled shyly and took hold of her hand. Biscuit appeared at the girl's feet, wagging his tail. Annie reached down and petted him gently.

When Gary dismissed the crowd to go to their sessions, Elizabeth took Annie into the church and sat down. The children were still getting settled in their seats when Elizabeth heard a voice behind her.

"Are you some teen prodigy or something?"

Elizabeth turned to look at Joe, trying not to blush. "No, I just like music. I'm usually nervous in front of people, but this was just a bunch of little kids. I didn't feel as nervous as I usually do."

"I play the guitar a little, but not as well as you play the piano. Still, we should get together and jam sometime," he said.

The Bible story teacher called the group to attention, and Elizabeth faced the front. *He wants to jam with me? Oh, Lord, what do I tell him? I wish he would leave me alone. Actually, I don't want him to leave me alone. What in the world is going on here, Lord?*

Her thoughts swirled, and she didn't catch a word of the Bible story. *Oh my goodness, Kate is right. I am swooning. I've never swooned over a boy. What is getting into me?* She was painfully aware of Joe's presence right behind her. *Lord, help me to know how to act. I don't even know if he's a Christian! And I'm only fourteen.*

The rest of the morning flew by. Joe, Maria, and Pedro jumped in to help where they could, and they seemed to really listen to the Bible stories and verses. Annie relaxed some and even talked to James as they worked together on a craft.

When it was time to clean up, Gary called Elizabeth to the front. "Why don't you play the keyboard for us while we work. I'll put this sign advertising our camp next to you, and as people walk by, maybe they'll notice and send their kids tomorrow. Here, I'll put up this sign for our mime show this evening, too."

Elizabeth agreed, and for the first time noticed the symbol at the bottom of the sign. "Gary, what is that?" she pointed.

"Oh, that's the symbol for the Kiwanis Club. They own the Fiesta Noche del Rio, the outdoor theater where we are performing each night. They like for their symbol to be on everything that advertises the theater. It helps with donations."

"Donations?" she asked.

"Yeah, they're a charity," Gary said, then called out some instructions to a couple of teenagers who were cleaning up.

Elizabeth turned and began playing the keyboard. She noticed Joe and Pedro talking to Gary and pointing to a guitar case. Gary smiled, nodded, and then knelt to open the case. The two of them approached the soundboard behind Elizabeth, and she tried to ignore them. People passing stopped and read the signs. Many of them stood for a few minutes, enjoying her upbeat music. The teenagers and some of the children sang along as they worked.

After a few moments, Elizabeth heard a bass guitar coming from behind her. Turning her head just a little, she saw it was Joe. A rhythmic clicking noise from the other side of her was Pedro. A drummer? He had two pencils, and was clicking away on the stair railing. It sounded good.

The three of them continued playing for a half hour. Surprisingly, Elizabeth didn't feel self-conscious. She got caught up in the music and just enjoyed herself.

Finally, they wrapped up their little concert and received light applause from the people gathered around. Unplugging the keyboard, she heard Pedro say, "That was so cool! We need a keyboardist for our band, Elizabeth. Too bad you don't live here."

"You have a band?" she asked, and Joe laughed.

"We want to have a band. So far it's just me with my borrowed guitar and Pedro with his pencils. We're both in the band at school, but we use the school's instruments. During the summer, we have trouble finding good instruments to play."

"What kind of music do you like to play?" Elizabeth asked.

"All kinds," said Joe. "Mostly rock 'n' roll. But I really

like what you're playing. I never knew Christian music could be so cool."

Elizabeth smiled. "Being a Christian is pretty cool," she told him.

Joe looked at his feet. "Yeah, my mom's always trying to get me to go to church. Maybe I'll have to try it."

Kate approached, Biscuit at her heels. "So, did you talk to them about. . .you know?" she asked Elizabeth.

Her question immediately got his attention. Maria and Pedro approached and joined the conversation.

"Talk to us about what?" asked Joe.

Elizabeth shot Kate a frustrated look, but Kate simply adjusted her glasses and smiled.

What is she up to? Elizabeth wondered. *We're supposed to check with Uncle Dan before we make any more plans.*

Just then, Elizabeth's mother waved to her. James was seated on the ground beside her, dangling his feet into the river. "Elizabeth, what are you girls planning to do for lunch? Your father and I want to go to the mall, if you're interested."

"Well, we told Uncle Dan we'd meet him after Bible Camp. If it's okay, we'd like to hang around here for a while," she told her mother.

"Okay," Mrs. Anderson said. She made sure Elizabeth had money for lunch, and waved good-bye. "We'll meet you back at the hotel at two o'clock," she called over her shoulder.

When she was gone, Joe asked her once again. "Talk to us about what?"

Kate spoke up. "We may need your help with a little project we're working on. But right now, Elizabeth and I have to meet someone. Why don't we meet you in an hour at the Rio Rio. You can order us some of those great tamales your mom was making yesterday."

The threesome agreed, and Elizabeth and Kate headed toward the hotel. "What was that about?" Elizabeth questioned. "I thought we were supposed to keep our mouths shut until we talked to Uncle Dan again!"

"My mistake," Kate apologized. "I saw you all deep in conversation and assumed that's what you were talking about. What were you talking about, by the way?"

Elizabeth smiled. "We were talking about music. Did you hear Joe playing the guitar? He's good."

"It's a match made in heaven," Kate teased, and Elizabeth reached over and pulled Kate's pink ball cap over her eyes. "Hey, stop that!" Kate called, straightening her cap.

Uncle Dan was waiting for them when they entered the lobby, and wasted no time in small talk. "I've been thinking about how we can catch these guys," he said. "Kate, didn't you say you brought a bag full of spy gizmos and gadgets?"

Kate nodded. "I have a bug we can plant to listen in on conversations. We thought we'd start with that."

"Perfect," said Uncle Dan. "I talked to Lyndel this morning—he's the owner of River City Cruises. He said the problems started a couple of weeks before Santa Anna Tours opened for business. I also found out that the owner of Santa Anna Tours has a history of illegal behavior. I'm not sure what he's capable of, so you girls need to stay safe. Don't go wandering off into any lonely alleys or tunnels. Stay on the Riverwalk, stay together, and stay where there is a crowd."

Elizabeth felt chills go up her spine. "This guy sounds dangerous."

"He's never been accused of anything violent—mostly petty theft and vandalism—but the bottom line is, he can't be trusted. We don't know what he's capable of. Can I trust you girls to act responsibly?"

The girls nodded, wide-eyed.

"Okay, then. Here's the plan," he said, and the three spent the next half hour plotting and planning.

●—●—●

At 1:15 p.m., Kate and Elizabeth spotted their friends seated at the Rio Rio.

Joe smiled at Elizabeth. "We were about to give up on you," he said. "Mom made this huge plate of tamales just for you, and I thought I would have to eat them myself."

"Don't you dare!" Elizabeth told him, and the group laughed. They made room for the two girls to sit down and politely joined Kate and Elizabeth as they prayed over their food.

Then, Maria leaned her elbows on the table, resting her

chin on her hands. "Joe said you wanted to talk to us about something," she said.

Elizabeth took a bite of the delicious tamales, and closed her eyes. "I have dreamed about these tamales. These are the best things I have ever tasted. Joe, do you think your mom would give me the recipe?"

He smiled. "We might be able to work something out. But first, you need to tell us what Kate was talking about earlier. What's the big secret?"

Kate swallowed her bite of tamale then leaned back in her chair. "Well, you remember those guys who chased us yesterday? We think they're the ones who are sabotaging the River City Cruise boats. But we may need your help to catch them."

The Plan

The three cousins leaned forward. "Sounds exciting. What do you need us to do?" asked Joe.

Elizabeth began filling them in on the plan. "We'd like to use all of you, or at least a couple of you, as scapegoats. We want to blame you, very loudly and in public, for the problems with the River City boats. Then, the real bad guys will think we're off their tails, when we'll actually be watching their every move."

Joe and Pedro looked at each other.

"What makes you think anyone would believe we had anything to do with it?" Joe asked. "We're innocent."

Maria burst into laughter. "Innocent? You? That's the funniest thing I've heard in a long time!" The girl looked at Elizabeth and Kate. "Trust me. Joe and Pedro have a reputation around here. Everyone would believe they did it."

Pedro's eyes grew large. "What do you mean, Joe and Pedro? What about you? You're right there, whenever we do anything!"

"Hey, all I do is watch! The water balloons, the rubber snakes. . ."

"Shhhhh! Stop talking. You'll make us look bad," he told his friends, glancing at Elizabeth. Maria laughed.

"If you're so innocent, why are you worried about looking bad? Your actions will speak for you," Elizabeth said. She finally had him cornered. He had practically admitted dropping the water balloon on her.

Joe leaned back in his chair and looked down at his hands. Finally, he looked up at Elizabeth, and she could see the hurt in his eyes. "So you think we're a bunch of hoodlums. Obviously, we'd be the best ones to take the rap for the vandalism."

Elizabeth felt terrible. Yes, she had thought they were hoodlums—in the beginning. But now she knew better, and she wouldn't want to hurt her new friends for anything.

The table grew quiet. She didn't know what to say.

After an awkward silence, Kate saved the day. "Look, nobody is accusing anybody of being hoodlums. If we thought you were hoodlums, we wouldn't ask you to help us. But don't even try to play innocent with us, Joe. We know all about your little games. Innocent fun? Perhaps. But you dropped that water balloon on Elizabeth, and everyone knows it. So why don't you just apologize and get it over with?"

Joe turned four shades of red, starting at his collar, then creeping up his chin, past his ears, and all the way to his head. After a moment, a smile crept onto his embarrassed face.

Elizabeth was taken off guard when he left his chair and knelt in front of her. The others snickered as they witnessed what was sure to be a great show.

"Señorita Anderson, it has been brought to my attention that, in my carelessness, I may have accidentally dropped a water balloon on your head," Joe told her. "I am so clumsy, and that balloon just slipped right out of my hands. I would never, ever intentionally drop a water balloon on someone as sweet and lovely as you. Will you please forgive me?"

Now, it was Elizabeth's turn to blush. Why couldn't she think of something clever to say? "Wait a minute," she said, rewinding his words in her mind. "Did you say it was an accident?"

The snickers got louder, and Joe just smiled.

"You expect me to believe that your dropping that water balloon on my head was an accident?" she continued. "I don't think so. Try your little apology again."

The group of witnesses laughed and waited to see what would happen next.

Joe laughed, too, but didn't back down. "Of course it was an accident, Elizabeth. I was aiming for the person in front of you!"

There. He had admitted it. He had dropped that water balloon on purpose, and Elizabeth wasn't sure she wanted to forgive him. She crossed her arms and tried to look angry, but it didn't work. The whole thing was too funny.

Finally, in a dramatic show of mercy, Elizabeth stood to her feet, took the long-handled teaspoon that rested on the table, and looked at Joe like a queen looking down on a peasant.

"Although you don't deserve my forgiveness, Señor Garcia, I shall grant it anyway. You"—she placed the teaspoon on one of his shoulders, like a scepter—"are pardoned." Lifting the teaspoon over his head, she touched his other shoulder.

The boy pretended to be overtaken with relief and gratitude, and the others at the table shook with laughter. Kate and Maria even had tears rolling down their cheeks, they were laughing so hard.

When they finally got under control, Pedro pulled the conversation back to its original topic. "So, tell us again what we can do to help you."

For the next half hour, they plotted and schemed over tortilla chips and tamales. When Kate and Elizabeth stood to leave, they felt both nervous and excited about the plan that would take place later that day.

●—●—●

Elizabeth sat in the overstuffed chair in the living area of their hotel room. Her feet were draped over the arm of the chair, and she casually twirled her long hair with her fingers.

"Mom and Dad, Kate and I were wondering if we could hang out with Uncle Dan this afternoon. He invited us to run some errands with him. Would that be okay?"

"Well, I just don't want you girls getting in his way," Mr. Anderson said. "But if he invited you, I suppose it's okay," he said.

Elizabeth rewarded him with a huge smile.

"I know how much you love your Uncle Dan, but he is coming to visit us in a couple of weeks. Not only that, but today we're going to the science museum, and we don't have anything like San Antonio's Science Museum in Amarillo. Are you sure you don't want to come with us?" said Mrs. Anderson.

Elizabeth nodded. "I know. The Science Museum is really fun, and I hate to miss it. But I'm excited about spending time with Uncle Dan. I think I'll enjoy that more."

"Okay. But stay with Uncle Dan, and stay out of trouble," her mother told her with a wink. "We'll probably go out to eat, too, so I'm not sure what time we'll be back. Keep your cell phone with you, and call us if you need anything."

"Yes, ma'am," Elizabeth called as her parents and James walked out the door.

"Whew, that was close," said Kate. "For a minute, I thought they were going to insist we go with them!"

"Well, they're gone now, and we don't have much time. Let's get the other Camp Club Girls on the phone, and see what they've come up with," Elizabeth told her.

Soon they had Bailey, Alex, and McKenzie on the

phone. Sydney was at her gymnastics class, so they'd have to fill her in later.

"Okay, everyone, it's crunch time. Since we talked to you last night, we've come up with a plan. In about forty-five minutes, we're going to stage a big scene, and my Uncle Dan and his friend, who owns the River City Cruises, are going to blame Joe and Pedro for all the vandalism that's been happening. Before that, we need to plant a listening device at the Santa Anna dock, but we're not sure how we'll do that. The Skipper knows who we are. They know we're onto them, so they'll be watching us. Any ideas?"

"What about having one of your new friends plant the device, before the whole scene plays out?" suggested Alex.

"That won't work," said Kate. "We were all together when those men chased us. They'll recognize them, too."

"Well then, what about Uncle Dan? They probably don't know who he is, do they?" asked McKenzie.

Elizabeth and Kate looked at each other. That could work.

"That's a good idea, McKenzie. Later, he'll go down there, strike up a conversation with the captain, and somehow hide the bug on the dock," Kate said.

"Then, Joe and Pedro can walk by," Elizabeth added. "Uncle Dan will call out, 'Hey, there they are!' and start accusing them of vandalizing the riverboats. They'll defend themselves for a few minutes, then leave. Then, Uncle Dan will change his mind about riding the boat, and leave, too."

"This is where the listening device comes in," Kate added. "After the whole scene plays out, we're hoping the captain and his sidekick will start talking and say something that will incriminate them."

"In-what-anate them?" asked Bailey.

"Incriminate," Kate said. "It means we hope they'll say something that will prove to us, and the police, that they are guilty of something."

"Well. . .it could work. Let's just hope Gilligan and the Skipper don't figure out that Uncle Dan is related to you," said Alex.

"Yep," said Elizabeth. "We've already talked about that. Kate and I will sit at a nearby café. Lots of people just sit and talk. We'll act oblivious to the whole thing."

"Well, be careful. You don't know what those men might do," said McKenzie.

Kate promised that yes, they would be careful.

Elizabeth looked at her watch. "We've got to get going. Uncle Dan's probably waiting for us. Oh! Did anyone research surgeries for a strawberry hemangioma birthmark?"

"I did, and I found out some interesting things," said McKenzie. "But we'll talk later. You go on, and call us as soon as the plan is executed. We want to hear every detail!"

The girls hung up, and after taking some deep breaths, Kate and Elizabeth headed downstairs to the lobby.

Uncle Dan was waiting for them, as expected. "Are you

ready to go?" he asked, a gleam of excitement in his eyes.

Elizabeth nodded. "We talked to our friends, and everything is set up. But we're hoping you can be the one to plant the listening device. The boat captain will be suspicious if he sees us hanging around his dock."

"That shouldn't be a problem for you. Just wait until the boat is on a tour, and the captain's not around. But I'll do it if you want."

"You'd better. There were two men, and even if the Skipper isn't around, I don't know where Gilligan might be," Elizabeth told him.

Uncle Dan nodded, and Kate handed him the device. He held it up to the light and examined it. "Wow. This is tiny. How far does the sound broadcast?"

Kate smiled proudly. "Elizabeth and I can be all the way at the other end of the Riverwalk, and we'll still hear the conversation."

"That's cool," he said.

Elizabeth looked out the glass lobby doors and saw Joe and Pedro standing near the Riverwalk. The lobby doors opened, and Maria walked in.

"The guys are ready to look guilty. They'll follow your cue," Maria told them, then returned to her cousins.

Uncle Dan eyed the group. "So they're the ones, huh? Let's hope they're good actors. I suppose it's good that they've never met me. It will seem more natural."

Something in the pit of Elizabeth's stomach told her

this wasn't going to go as planned. But she kept quiet. They had gone to all this trouble; she couldn't see the point in backing out now.

"You girls go find a place to sit and wait. I suggest you go to that little ice cream parlor with the balcony. If you sit up high, you'll be able to see us better," he suggested.

"Ice cream parlor?" asked Kate. "Sounds good to me. I'm starved!"

Elizabeth laughed. "Let's go," she said. "Uncle Dan, we're turning the listening device on now. Give us five minutes, and then tell us when you're leaving the lobby. You won't be able to hear us, but we'll hear you."

Uncle Dan nodded, and Kate and Elizabeth exited the lobby, trying to ignore their four friends standing outside. The last thing they needed was for the captain or his friend to see them together again.

For a split second, Elizabeth glanced at Joe. She couldn't seem to stop herself. He was watching her! She looked away, and led Kate to the ice cream parlor. Together, they climbed the steep stairs. "You go in and order, and I'll stay here on the balcony. This table is perfect. Look! We have a clear shot of the boat dock. We'll be able to see everything."

"Okay," agreed Kate. "I'll go get our ice cream. What do you want?"

"Anything chocolate," Elizabeth replied as she sat down.

Kate soon returned, and the girls were taking their first bites of ice cream when Elizabeth spotted something.

"Kate, look!" She pointed to a small shoe-shine booth. There, enjoying a shoe shine, was the Skipper. He was only a few yards from his boat dock, but his back was to it.

Uncle Dan's voice came over the tiny speaker. "Leaving the lobby, heading for the boat dock." The girls watched as Uncle Dan rolled his wheelchair to the railing as if to wait in the ticket line. He grabbed onto the railing as if he needed it for support, and Elizabeth smiled. She knew he was actually planting the listening device. The magnetic back clung securely to the underside of the metal railing— they had tested it earlier.

The Skipper approached with his newly shined shoes. He reached out to help Uncle Dan, and smiled.

"Welcome to Santa Anna Tours! How can I help you?" he asked.

So far, so good, thought Elizabeth.

"I'm thinking about taking one of your tours. But I'm a little hesitant," Uncle Dan told the man.

The captain lifted his eyebrows. "Oh? Why is that?"

"I've noticed a lot of the boats are breaking down. As you can see, since I'm in a wheelchair, it isn't easy for me to get on and off the boats. I certainly don't want to take the chance of getting myself or my chair wet."

"Oh, no need to worry. Santa Anna Tours has a perfect record. It's the other boat company that has had all the problems," the man said.

"I've heard that vandalism is suspected," Uncle Dan

said. The other man suddenly looked uncomfortable.

"I think I may know who is behind the vandalism, too," Uncle Dan continued.

The captain looked surprised. "Oh, really? Who might that be?"

Uncle Dan leaned closer to the man.

He is such a great actor! thought Elizabeth. *He should be on stage!*

"Some teenagers have been wandering around here, and they look like they're up to no good. There are two boys and a girl, and I don't trust them. If I were you, I'd watch out for—hey! There they are now!" Uncle Dan pointed, and the captain turned to see Joe, Pedro, and Maria walking past.

CHAPTER 9

Dog-napped!

Elizabeth and Kate licked their ice cream cones and watched the scene below, still listening on their tiny speaker. It was almost like watching a movie.

"Hey, you there!" Uncle Dan called out. "Didn't I see you at the other boat dock? You looked like you were up to no good. I think you've been messing with all the boats!"

The teenagers stopped, looking like they'd been caught. *Perfect,* thought Elizabeth.

"I don't know anything about any boats," said Joe defensively, and the other two agreed.

Uncle Dan wheeled his chair forward. "You'd better stay away from here. I'm onto you, and if I see you hanging around, making trouble, I'll call the police!"

So far, so good, thought Elizabeth. Some ice cream dripped from her cone, and Biscuit quickly cleaned it up.

Uncle Dan and the teens exchanged a few more angry words before the threesome moved on. Uncle Dan looked at the Skipper and said, "I think I'll pass on that ride. I'm going to call the police and report my suspicions right now."

The captain shook Uncle Dan's hand. "Thank you, sir. You're a good citizen. If more people would report hoodlums instead of just letting them wander around getting into trouble, we'd all be better off."

Elizabeth caught a glimpse of someone in the shadows, beneath the bridge. *It was Gilligan!* He seemed to listen to the conversation between Uncle Dan and the captain.

The hairs on Biscuit's back stood up, and he gave a low, throaty growl. Kate grabbed his collar. "Easy, boy," she whispered.

Uncle Dan began to wheel away. When his back was turned, the girls saw the captain motion for his sidekick to come closer.

"It looks like the heat is off, for a while. That guy thinks those teenagers have caused River City's problems. He's going to call the police," the Skipper told his partner.

Gilligan laughed. "That's perfect. And while everyone is focused on them, we can make another move."

Kate and Elizabeth looked at each other, wide-eyed. This was going exactly as planned! Now, if the recorder had worked correctly, all they'd have to do was take the recording to the police.

They were startled when a voice below them yelled, "Kate, Elizabeth! What are y'all doing up there? Come down and join us!"

It was Gary, and his loud voice echoed on the buildings around them. To the left and the right, tourists turned to see who Elizabeth and Kate were. The Skipper and Gilligan turned, too. Elizabeth locked eyes with the Skipper and realized he recognized her.

Just then, Gary spotted Uncle Dan, who was trying to wheel back into the hotel lobby. "Dan! Over here! I just spotted your niece and her friend. We're going to rent a riverboat. Do all of you want to come?"

Oh no. Did Gary just point out to the whole world. . . and to those men. . .that I'm Uncle Dan's niece? That can't be good.

All of a sudden, the Skipper's face went white. His jaw clenched, and he seemed to realize he'd been duped. "Hey, you!" he called out to Uncle Dan.

Without warning, Biscuit leaped from the low balcony and dashed straight for the Skipper! The little dog bared his teeth and growled.

"Why, you little mutt. . . ," the man said, kicking at Biscuit. The little dog backed up, but continued to growl.

"Hey!" Uncle Dan yelled, wheeling his chair around. "Cut it out!"

The Skipper looked around at all the witnesses and took a deep breath. Rage flooded his eyes. But he pasted on a smile and said, "Sorry about that, folks. I get a little nervous when a dog bares his teeth at me."

By this time Kate and Elizabeth were on the ground, and Uncle Dan wheeled up beside Elizabeth. He didn't say a word, just gave the Skipper a steely-eyed stare. Even in a wheelchair, Uncle Dan offered a powerful presence. He was a war veteran. A war hero. He'd faced things far more dangerous than a crooked riverboat owner.

The Skipper held eye contact with Uncle Dan, then turned. "Well, folks, the show's over. Now, who wants to go for a ride?"

The line that had been forming dispersed, causing the captain more frustration. But he continued to stand there, smiling and nodding. "Come back another time," he said weakly.

About that time, Kate looked around. "Where's Biscuit?" she asked.

Elizabeth looked to the spot where Biscuit had stood moments earlier, but the little dog was nowhere in sight.

"Biscuit?" Kate called. "Biscuit, where are you?" Her voice came out in a squeak.

Elizabeth put her hand on Kate's shoulder and said, "He was just here a minute ago. I'm sure he's around here somewhere. The captain doesn't have him, and—" She looked around for Gilligan. He was gone, too.

Oh no! It can't be! God, please don't let that man have Biscuit! God, please keep Biscuit safe!

Soon, everyone around was calling for the little dog. Even strangers were looking beneath restaurant tables and in shadowy corners, hoping for a sign of Biscuit.

Elizabeth looked at Uncle Dan, who had his eye on the captain and his empty boat. "Are you thinking what I'm thinking?" she whispered.

"If you're thinking we need to keep an eye on that man and his sidekick, then yes," he said. "Do you have the recorder? Let's go see if we got a good recording of the whole thing. Then we'll come up with a plan to find Biscuit."

The recorder! In the excitement, had they left it on the table at the ice cream shop?

"Kate!" she called, scanning the crowd.

She spotted Kate next to Gary, who was trying to calm her. "We'll find him. There were too many people around for him to have just disappeared. Surely someone saw something!"

Kate continued to look through the crowds. "That man took him. I know he did," she told her youth minister.

Gary looked confused. "That man? What man? What are you talking about?"

Elizabeth interrupted their conversation. "Excuse me, Kate. I think that little recorder might lead us to Biscuit. Do you have it?"

For a moment, Kate looked dazed, as if she didn't comprehend. Then understanding dawned, and she began feeling in her pockets. "The recorder! Oh no! When Biscuit jumped off the balcony, I just went after him. I think I left it on the table!"

The girls ran to the ice cream shop. They took the low, curved steps two at a time, and found a mother with two small boys sitting at their table.

"Excuse me," Elizabeth approached the woman politely. "My friend and I left something at this table. Did you see a small, round, black device by any chance?"

The woman shook her head. "No, I'm sorry. I didn't see anything," she said.

"Is this what you're looking for?" asked one of the boys. He held up the recorder. "I found it in the chair. It's really cool! I've been pushing the buttons."

Pushing the buttons? Oh no!

Elizabeth took the recorder from the boy and smiled. "Thank you," she told him.

The girls went down the stairs and found Gary waiting for them at the bottom. "Kate? What man? I think you need to tell me what you're talking about."

Kate sighed, but said nothing. Elizabeth knew her friend was too distraught to think clearly.

"Gary, why don't you come with us? We're going to talk to my Uncle Dan. We'll explain everything." Elizabeth led Kate through the maze of tourists.

They pushed open one of the sparkly, double glass doors of the hotel and found Uncle Dan waiting for them. "Did you find it?" he asked.

"Yes," she answered. "But there's no telling what kind of shape it's in. A little boy had it. He was about James's age. And he was pushing all the buttons."

Uncle Dan pushed the PLAY button, and heard a child's laughter. Then he heard a woman's voice saying, "Be careful, Joshua. You don't want your ice cream cone to fall on the floor." Then, more laughter.

Great, thought Elizabeth. "What are we going to do now?" she asked.

Kate spoke up, seeming to have gained control of her emotions. "We're going to find Biscuit! That's what we're going to do."

Gary put his arm on Kate's shoulder. "We'll do all we can to find Biscuit. But first, I think you need to tell me what's going on."

●—●—●

An hour later, a massive search party had been formed. Gary organized the teens from Kate's youth group into teams, and they were instructed to search the east side of the Riverwalk. Joe, Pedro, and Maria were to search the west side leading to the Alamo. Uncle Dan, Kate, and Elizabeth decided to go through the underground tunnel that led to the mall.

Before they left, however, Uncle Dan turned to Kate. "I need you to bring all of your spy gadgets. You never know what we might need. I have a couple of gadgets of my own. You go get your equipment, and I'll meet you back here in five minutes."

The girls wasted no time. While Kate was piling the gadgets into her backpack, Elizabeth sent a text to the other Camp Club Girls: BISCUIT MISSING. SEARCHING NOW. PRAY.

She pressed the SEND button, then did a little praying of her own—out loud, so Kate could hear. "Dear Father, we don't know where Biscuit is, but You do. Please keep him safe. If those men have him, please don't let them hurt him. And please help us to find him. Soon."

Kate wiped a tear from her cheek and whispered, "Amen." She zipped up her backpack, and they headed to the lobby. In the elevator, she said, "Elizabeth, I'm scared. I'm really scared. This is even worse than at camp, when Biscuit was missing. Then, he just ran away. This time, I really think he was kidnapped. What if. . ."

Elizabeth put her arm around her friend's shoulder. "We're not going to think about 'what if.' We've asked God to help us find Biscuit, and to keep him safe. Now, we just have to trust God to do that. Remember Mark 11:24, 'Therefore I tell you, whatever you ask for in prayer, believe that you have received it, and it will be yours.' "

Kate nodded. "I know. I want to believe. But in this case, that's easier said than done."

"I know what you mean," said Elizabeth. "I guess if faith in God were easy, more people would believe."

"I wish I'd left that tracking device on his collar!" Kate said. "If only I hadn't taken it off when I got here!"

The elevator doors opened into the lobby, where Uncle Dan was waiting. After a quick show-and-tell of the gadgets, they headed toward the mall. Instead of the usual way, however, Uncle Dan led them through a tiny door in the side of one of the buildings.

"Where are we going?" asked Elizabeth.

"We're still going to the mall," Uncle Dan answered. "But if Biscuit was truly taken, the kidnappers wouldn't have him right out in the open. There are dozens of these passageways between the mall and the Riverwalk, and few people even know about them. They were built so store owners would have a back way in and out of their stores, but they are hardly used." He pointed to a series of doors along the side of the passageway. "These rooms are mostly used for storage, and each one has a door on the other side leading to one of the stores. Most of the store owners prefer to go through the mall, and get to their storage rooms from there."

"I don't blame them," said Elizabeth. "There's something creepy about this. . .I wouldn't want to walk through here every day, either."

"I think we need to search these passageways," said Uncle Dan. "I think it's the only way that guy could have escaped unseen. I don't know where all the entrances are; most were built to blend in with the landscape of the Riverwalk. They're difficult to see, if you don't already know where they are."

"Wow," whispered Kate. "It's like we've just walked into a spy movie. Only it's real."

Uncle Dan stopped his wheelchair, turning to face them. "Elizabeth, you have your cell phone, right?"

Elizabeth nodded.

"You two go on into the mall, and see what you can find. Remember, you're not looking for Biscuit, though if you find him, that's great. You're looking for doors to these tunnels. Look around, ask around, see what you can find out. Call me as soon as you know something."

"What then?" asked Elizabeth.

Uncle Dan pulled out a long telescope-looking device. "This is a peephole reverser. It allows you to look the other way through a peephole in a door, so you can see what's going on inside the room. We have to use these sometimes in the hotel rooms, if we think someone is in danger. If you can find the doors, even if they are locked, we can look inside. As long as there is a peephole, that is."

The girls' eyes grew round. "Cool!" Elizabeth said.

"Why don't you do the honors?" Uncle Dan handed Elizabeth the device and gestured to the doors. Kate was too short to reach the peephole, and Uncle Dan was out of reach, as well.

Elizabeth went from door to door, looking inside the rooms. Most of the rooms were dark, but a couple of them revealed only stacks of cardboard boxes. One had toys and stuffed animals on shelves, and she knew that was the toy store. Before long, she had looked through all the doors. No Biscuit in sight.

"Do you want me to keep this?" Elizabeth asked her uncle.

"No. If you're caught with it, you'll have a hard time

explaining. Thieves use these to check out the places they want to rob." Uncle Dan returned the device to his duffel bag and said, "Remember, you've got to think like the bad guys. Where would they go? What would they do? Go and see what you can find out, and meet me back here in half an hour. I'm going to find some of the shop owners and ask some questions. Maybe somebody saw something."

Kate and Elizabeth headed into the mall. After a few steps, Kate stopped. "Wait. Take this," she said, holding out a small pack of gum.

"Oh, no thanks," said Elizabeth. "I'm not in the mood for gum right now."

Kate continued holding the gum out. "Take it," she said. Then, moving a little closer, she whispered, "It's a walkie-talkie. See the button? I have one, too." She held up another pack of gum. "This way, if we accidentally get separated, we can communicate."

Elizabeth's eyes grew wide, and she examined the small rectangular device. It looked exactly like a pack of gum. But sure enough, there was a tiny button on the back.

"Kate, you are full of surprises," she told her friend, tucking the *gum* into her pocket.

The two girls had only passed a couple of stores when they spotted another passageway. Kate tested it, and sure enough, it was unlocked. "Should we go in?"

"Uncle Dan has the peephole reverser. He said to call when we found something." Elizabeth pulled out her cell phone, ready to call Uncle Dan, when she heard someone calling her name. She looked up to find Joe, Pedro, and Maria coming toward her.

"There you are!" Joe said, looking out of breath. "We've been looking all over for you! Come with us. We think we may have found something."

Maria grabbed Kate's arm, and said, "Come on! You've got to listen to this."

"Have you found Biscuit? Do you know where my dog is?" Kate asked, hope filling her face.

"Just come on!" said Pedro, pulling Elizabeth along behind him. They took off, jogging when possible, slowing to a walk when they were in crowds. They had gone almost the length of the mall when Joe gestured to a hidden doorway. "This way!" he said.

The six young people entered the doorway, and Joe led them to a small round hole in the wall. The rim of some PVC pipe was barely visible. Joe leaned and placed his ear against the pipe, then stepped back.

"Listen," he said to Kate.

She stepped forward and placed her ear against the pipe. Relief flooded her face. "It's Biscuit! He's okay! Listen, Beth! It's Biscuit!"

Elizabeth stepped forward and placed her ear to the pipe. Sure enough, she heard Biscuit's familiar howling.

"This is great!" Elizabeth cried. "So. . .where is he? Where can we find him?"

Their new friends looked at each other. "Well. . .um. . . we don't exactly know. These pipes run all through the mall, and even to other places on the Riverwalk. He could be anywhere."

CHAPTER 10

Searching for Biscuit

Elizabeth pulled out her cell phone. "Let me call Uncle Dan. He was in charge of search-and-rescue missions in Vietnam. He'll know what to do." She dialed the number and held the phone to her ear.

Nothing.

She dialed again, with the same results. "I can't get a signal. I guess these tunnels are too closed in. Come on, Kate. Let's go find Uncle Dan."

Kate stood her ground. "I'm not going anywhere until I know how to find Biscuit. I'm staying right here where I can hear him. Hey! I wonder if he can hear me?"

She cupped her hands around the pipe and called into the hole, "Biscuit! Biscuit, it's me. Calm down, boy. We're going to find you."

She placed her ear to the hole and reported, "He heard me! He's whimpering, but he's not howling anymore. He knows we're on our way."

Elizabeth placed her phone back in her pocket. They had no choice. They would have to split up. Someone had to go figure out where the other end of that pipe was, and Kate wasn't moving. "Okay. You stay here. I'll try to find Uncle Dan. If I can't find him, I'll at least find out what's on the other side of this wall. Whatever you do, don't go anywhere. The last thing we need is to lose you, too."

Elizabeth left the group behind, but she wasn't surprised when she heard footsteps behind her. She turned to find Joe.

"I'm coming, too. Maria and Pedro can stay with Kate. There's safety in numbers, you know," Joe told her.

She nodded and kept walking. She wasn't sure if she was glad for the company or not. *I don't have time to be distracted by you, Mr. Charm. I have a dog to find and a mystery to solve.*

As if reading her mind, Joe spoke up again. "I won't get in your way. I'm here to help."

They turned the corner to see what was on the other side of that wall. A shoe store. Elizabeth entered the store and headed straight to the back wall.

"May I help you?" asked a young sales clerk.

Elizabeth didn't respond, just kept studying the wall behind the shoes.

"Uh, no thank you. We're just looking," Joe answered the woman, and she moved to another customer.

"What are you thinking, Elizabeth?" he asked her.

"I wonder if there's a way we can get into those storage rooms. Legally, I mean. If we had access to the back entrances, it would be easier to explore the tunnels. As it is, we don't even know where all the entrances are," she told him.

A slow smile spread across his face, lighting up his green eyes.

Those are the nicest eyes I've ever seen, thought Elizabeth. *Stop it! Do not get distracted!*

She forced herself to look back at the shoes.

"I have an idea. Follow me," Joe told her, and led the way out of the store. Elizabeth followed him two stores down, to a music store. In the window hung a sign that read HELP WANTED.

He approached the counter and asked the clerk for a job application form. While he waited, he looked at Elizabeth and smiled. "I've been wanting a job here, anyway. Now maybe we can kill two birds with one stone."

Elizabeth smiled. She had to hand it to him. It was a brilliant idea. Noticing a shiny grand piano in a corner of the store, she approached it. Almost reverently, she sat at the bench.

Wow, she thought. *I'd love to have a piano like this.*

Gingerly, she pressed one of the keys, and it let out a sweet, pure tone that only a true musician could appreciate.

"Go ahead. Give it a try," said the clerk.

"Really?" she asked in disbelief. "You don't mind if I play it?"

The clerk smiled, and Elizabeth settled in front of the keys. Within moments, she was lost in Mozart's "Sonata in C." Then, without warning, she transitioned into a blues scale and began playing an old Elvis Presley hit. Her music was beginning to draw a crowd when she heard a beeping sound. *Where is that coming from?*

She continued to play, but the beeping persisted. Suddenly, she realized it was coming from her pocket. *The gum!*

She abruptly stopped playing. A few people in the crowd groaned, then left. Elizabeth smiled, stood, and walked behind a large set of drums. Pulling the walkie-talkie gum gadget from her pocket, she pressed the tiny button and whispered, "Hello?"

"Elizabeth! Where have you been? I've been beeping you for five minutes!" Kate's voice came over the tiny speaker.

"Uh, sorry. I, uh, didn't hear you. What's going on?"

"There were voices. Human ones. I couldn't make out everything they said, but one of them sounded like the Skipper," Kate told her. "They're gone now. I can still hear Biscuit, so I know he's okay—for now. But we don't know what those men are capable of. We've got to find him. Soon."

Elizabeth stood behind the drums, peering into the mall beyond the store entrance. "I know. We'll find him. We just have to believe that."

As she waited for Kate's reply, she spotted something in the crowd—or rather, someone. A tall, awkward-looking man, pressing his way through the shoppers. *Was that. . .it was Gilligan!*

"Kate! Gotta go. Stay put!" Elizabeth said, and took off

through the maze of people, after the man.

"Elizabeth! Wait up!" Joe called, but Elizabeth didn't slow down. Joe caught up with her and asked, "Did I just see you talking to a pack of gum?"

Elizabeth pointed. "That's the man! We have to follow him. He may lead us to Biscuit!"

A crowd was forming ahead, and the man pressed through it. Elizabeth walked as fast as her long legs would carry her, trying to keep an eye on him. But by the time she approached the crowd, she'd lost him. A teenage girl was in the center of the crowd passing out free ice cream samples. But suddenly, she had no appetite.

"Did you see where he went?" asked Joe, and Elizabeth turned. She had almost forgotten he was with her.

"No," she replied.

"Well, he didn't seem to be carrying anything. Wherever he is, I don't think Biscuit is with him. Maybe we should go back and find the others," Joe suggested.

"I agree. But first, I need to make a phone call."

●—●—●

Back at the hotel, Kate, Elizabeth, Maria, and Pedro entered Uncle Dan's suite. Joe had been hired at the music store, and had been asked to rearrange some boxes in the storage area. With a discreet nod, the boy had assured his friends he would find out what he could with his new access.

This suite was Uncle Dan's home for as long as he worked for the Palacio del Rio. It had everything he needed:

kitchen, living room, bedroom, bathroom, even a guest room, though most of his guests ended up staying in another hotel room.

Kate paced back and forth. "I can't believe I just left Biscuit there. I should go back. He needs to hear my voice. It calms him."

Uncle Dan looked at her compassionately. "I know you didn't want to leave him. But we still don't know where he is. I think we need to pull an all-out spy mission on the Skipper. But he'll suspect us, so we have to look like we're going about business as usual.

"Kate, let's get a look at all of your gadgets. We'll compare yours to mine, and together, I'm sure we'll be able to find Biscuit and put those men in jail before you know it."

Kate emptied her backpack onto Uncle Dan's coffee table while he wheeled into his bedroom. A moment later, he reappeared with a hard black suitcase. Scooting Kate's gadgets to the side, he set the suitcase down and opened it. Inside, the suitcase looked like something from a spy movie.

Together, Kate and Uncle Dan had miniature cameras and recorders, trackers, voice distortion tools, telescopes of various shapes and sizes, and more.

Elizabeth picked up one of the tiny devices and looked at it. "I wish we could figure out a way to track the Skipper. But to do that, we'd have to attach a tracking device to him. And I don't know how we can do that."

Pedro spoke up. "I have an idea," he said. "I know a place the Skipper visits several times a day."

• — • — •

Elizabeth and Kate had a perfect view from their private balcony, and they watched breathlessly as Pedro pulled the cap low over his head and sat in the shoe-shine booth. His friend had been happy to take a break and let Pedro take over the business for a few minutes.

Sure enough, right on schedule, the Skipper showed up. He didn't even look at Pedro! He just dropped a few coins in the jar and placed his right foot on the stand. Pedro worked diligently at shining first the right shoe, then the left one.

Though the girls couldn't see the details, they noticed Pedro took a bit longer with the left shoe. Finally, they saw him give his rag a final pop, and the Skipper walked away without so much as a nod.

Kate held up her tiny tracking screen, and sure enough, it sprang to life. The tiny red dot was moving—barely—as the Skipper marched to the boat.

Elizabeth texted the other Camp Club Girls, who had been briefly informed of the situation: MISSION ACCOMPLISHED. Or at least, Phase One had been accomplished. Within moments, her cell phone rang, and she knew it was them, standing by on a conference call.

"It went off without a flaw," Elizabeth spoke without even saying hello.

Kate picked up her cell phone, which was also ringing, and joined the conversation.

"I can't believe Elizabeth's uncle wants us to lie low," complained Kate. "Biscuit is out there. I need to go rescue him."

"You have a better chance of rescuing him if Gilligan and the Skipper think you're backing off. You know he's okay—for now. But if they feel like you're putting pressure on them, you don't know what they'll do," said McKenzie.

"McKenzie's right," said Alex. "The reason they kidnapped Biscuit in the first place was to warn you to back off. You want them to think you've taken their warning."

"You know, guys, I remembered something I learned in nature study, and I've pulled up some sound travel research on my computer," Sydney said. "Sometimes, when traveling through a tunnel—or a pipe—the sound can become distorted. It can sound like Biscuit is close, when actually, he could be very far away."

"And your point is?" Kate asked, frustrated.

"Just that you may not want to limit your search to the mall. He could be on the other side of the river," Sydney continued.

"Yes, but I saw Gilligan in the mall, just after Kate heard voices," Elizabeth said.

"Did he know you were looking for him?" asked Bailey.

"Of course he knew we were looking for him. He took my dog!" Kate cried.

Everyone was silent for a few moments. Finally,

Elizabeth said, "So you think he was purposely trying to lead us in the wrong direction?"

"I don't know," said Sydney. "I just don't want you to zero in on one area, while Biscuit may be in an entirely different location."

Kate groaned. "Poor Biscuit! My poor baby. He's all alone and scared. What if we never find him?"

"We'll find him," Elizabeth said with a confidence she didn't feel.

"How can you be so sure?" Kate voiced the question on everyone's mind.

"Because God is good," said Elizabeth.

"Well, it sure doesn't feel like He's good right now," said Kate.

Elizabeth did not have an answer for her. Then, a verse popped into her mind.

"For I am the LORD, your God, who takes hold of your right hand and says to you, Do not fear; I will help you," she said. "Isaiah 41:13. We'll find him, because God will help us."

There was a knock at the door. Elizabeth set her phone on the bed and cracked the door to find Gary. Behind him was Charis, the girl who taught the Bible stories.

"We've looked everywhere," Gary said. "We've got to stop and get ready for tonight's performance."

"Tell Kate we're sorry," said Charis.

With a nod, Elizabeth softly closed the door. She turned to find Kate behind her. Kate had heard every word.

Elizabeth picked up her phone and called the Camp Club Girls on a conference call. She told the others about Biscuit, and they were silent for a few moments.

Finally, Bailey changed the subject. "Hey, who was it that had news on the strawberry?"

"Oh yeah. The strawberry birthmark," said Sydney. "The strawberry nevus is quite common, and as many as one in ten babies have them. They usually disappear in early childhood."

"That's great news!" said Elizabeth. "Maybe Annie's birthmark will just go away, all by itself!"

"Probably not," continued Sydney. "The strawberry hemangioma is a little different. If the birthmark continues to grow, it's probably a hemangioma, and it won't go away on its own. Didn't her mother mention that it was growing?"

"Yes," Elizabeth replied, disappointed.

"This is terrible," said McKenzie. "That poor little girl!"

"There's more," Sydney told them. "If it's not taken care of, it has the potential, down the road, to become cancerous."

Elizabeth thought of sweet little Annie. *God, no. Please don't let her get cancer.*

"I don't know how much more bad news I can take," said Kate, flopping on her bed.

"Well, there is some good news," said Sydney. "There is an organization called the Kiwanis Club. They have chapters all over the U.S., so I'm sure San Antonio has one."

"Hey, I saw something about them on *Walker, Texas Ranger*! Don't they do things to help little children?" exclaimed Alex.

"Yes," Sydney replied. "They help improve the quality of children's lives, especially young children. Each chapter tries to sponsor at least one service project per year. Maybe you can hook Annie up with a local Kiwanis Club. Maybe they'll help."

Elizabeth couldn't believe what she was hearing. "Kate!" she said, causing Kate to jump from her spot on the bed.

"What?" answered the startled girl.

"Do you remember seeing that sign on the stage where the teens perform each night?"

Kate looked thoughtful. "I remember seeing a sign, but I didn't pay much attention."

"It's a Kiwanis sign!" exclaimed Elizabeth. "They must own the Fiesta Noche!"

"Come to think of it, Gary did say we were renting it from some organization. Hey, wouldn't that be cool if that money ended up helping Annie?"

"Thanks, Sydney. You're the best!" Elizabeth said. "All of you are the best! Kate, what time is it?"

"It's dinnertime," said Kate. "But for once, I'm not really hungry."

Elizabeth patted her friend's shoulder. "Let's go watch the show. Afterward, we'll talk to Gary, and maybe he can put us in touch with the Kiwanis director. Then we'll search for Biscuit some more."

Kate nodded slowly. Elizabeth wished she could take this burden from her friend.

McKenzie spoke up then. "Kate, it will be okay. I have this feeling it will all work out, and you'll find Biscuit. Just like at camp, remember?"

Bailey chimed in. "Yeah, and remember the verse Elizabeth told us, about God helping us!"

"And we'll all be praying," Alex said. "I'll bet you'll find Biscuit by tomorrow."

With a few more encouraging words, the girls said good-bye and promised to be in touch soon.

Elizabeth started to leave, but Kate stopped her. "Wait," she said. "Let me check my blog first."

Once again, there was a comment waiting. Kate nearly lost her balance when she read what it said: *"Back off. If you want to see your dog alive again, you'll keep your mouths shut."*

Elizabeth reached an arm out to steady her friend. "Don't worry, Kate. They won't hurt him. He's their bargaining chip," she said with more confidence than she felt.

Kate took a deep breath. She grabbed the tracking device, and the girls left the room without looking at it. But in the elevator, they couldn't help but notice. The device was lighting up like a Christmas tree.

The Skipper was on the move.

The Girls Confess!

Kate pressed the ground floor button on the elevator again and again, as if that would make the elevator move faster. "Hurry up! Stop being so slow!"

Elizabeth looked through the window, scanning the area, looking for signs of the navy blue captain's hat. Finally, she saw it.

"Calm down, Kate. He's getting a hot dog," she said. She watched the man pay for his snack, then turn back toward his boat.

Kate held up the tracker again, and sure enough, the tiny red dot was returning to its original location.

"Whew," she said. "I guess we need to keep a closer watch. He could have been from here to Timbuktu by now!"

The elevator doors opened, and the girls saw Uncle Dan talking to a gray-haired couple, obviously hotel guests. When they left, the girls approached. Kate held up the tracker so he could see.

"This is perfect," she told him.

Uncle Dan looked at the device. "Pedro and Maria

stopped by after the tracker was in place. They were headed to the mall to see if Joe'd learned anything. They said they'd check back later."

"We're going to watch the kids' performance tonight. We need a change of pace, and we have another project we're working on. We have the tracker, and we can leave if the Skipper does anything out of the ordinary," Elizabeth told him.

Uncle Dan nodded. "I wish I could help you more, girls, but I'm back on duty. I think you're safe for another couple of hours. The Skipper will continue to give tours until after dark. And I have another surprise for you," he said with a smirk.

The girls looked at each other, then back at Uncle Dan.

"While Pedro was shoe-shining, I was doing a little detective work. There is now a mini-transmitter on the back of the Skipper's steering wheel." He handed the girls a tiny speaker. "You can now listen to him give tours . . . or anything else he may talk about when he's on or near the boat. This little baby will pick up any conversation for about twenty feet."

Kate looked at the device, eyebrows lifted. "Wow. This is the latest model, isn't it? I've been wanting this one."

Uncle Dan smiled, then turned to greet a new set of customers. The girls waved, then headed out the glass doors.

"I guess this means we can relax for a little while. The Skipper will give tours, and we'll be able to see when he moves, and hear what he says," Elizabeth said.

Kate held the tiny device to her ear. "Sounds like he's giving a tour now." Looking at the tracker, she watched the red dot move slowly across the screen. "His movement will be slow and steady as long as he's on the boat. I guess we can watch it, and if the pattern changes, we'll know something's up."

The girls were almost to the Fiesta Noche when they ran into Elizabeth's parents. James was wearing a hat shaped like a tyrannosaurus Rex.

"Roar!" he said, and Elizabeth pretended to be afraid.

"There you girls are," said Mr. Anderson. "We were just about to call you. You missed a lot of excitement this afternoon! They had a special dinosaur exhibit at the museum. Did you have a nice time with Uncle Dan?"

Elizabeth glanced at Kate, who was looking at her shoes. "Well, um. . .we had some excitement of our own," she said. "Biscuit's missing."

"What?" exclaimed Mr. and Mrs. Anderson in unison. "How did that happen? When?"

"It happened a few hours ago. We've been looking for him ever since," said Elizabeth.

"Why didn't you call us?" asked Elizabeth's mother.

"Uncle Dan has been helping us look for him, and I didn't want to bother you," said Elizabeth.

Mr. Anderson looked from Elizabeth to Kate, then back to Elizabeth. Was that suspicion on his face?

Elizabeth's mother put her arm around Kate, pulling her into a hug. "You know we'll do all we can to find him, sweetie," she said. Kate nodded.

"Are you two girls involved in another mystery of some sort?" asked Mr. Anderson.

Just then, Elizabeth spotted Gary talking to an older gentleman. He was handing him an envelope. "Excuse me, Dad. I really need to speak to Gary. Do you mind?"

Mr. Anderson excused his daughter, and Elizabeth politely approached the two adults. Kate followed behind, her eyes on the tracker.

When there was an appropriate break in the conversation, Elizabeth said, "Hi Gary. I need to ask you a question. Are you renting this stage from the Kiwanis Club?"

Gary looked surprised. "Yes, we are. This is the Kiwanis representative, right here, Mr. Adams." He looked at the gentleman and said, "Let me introduce you to a couple of my biggest helpers, Elizabeth and Kate."

"Nice to meet you," said the girls, each shaking the man's hand.

"Are you interested in joining the Kiwanis Club?" he asked them.

"Possibly," Elizabeth replied. "But I'm also interested in letting you know about a possible service project," she said.

"Wonderful!" the man told her. "We're always looking for chances to help kids. Tell me about your idea."

Elizabeth began pouring out Annie's story, and the man

gestured to a small bench. They sat down and kept talking. Soon, Elizabeth's parents joined them. Before long, the man was nodding and smiling.

"Yes," he said. "This sounds like exactly the kind of project we've been looking for. When can I meet Annie?"

"She's been coming to the Bible club every morning at the church at La Villita. Can you come tomorrow morning?"

"I'll be there. It may be late morning, but I will be there before your Bible club is over." He shook her hand, then Kate's, and said, "Thank you, girls. I love to see young people who care about others, and who want to help. You're exactly the kind of girls we need in the Kiwanis organization."

Elizabeth's parents smiled at the girls. "This will make such a difference in Annie's life. I'm proud of you girls," said Mrs. Anderson.

"I am, too," said Elizabeth's dad. "But I still feel like you're not telling me something. Unfortunately, I'm starved. Are you girls hungry?"

"No, sir," Kate and Elizabeth responded.

Mr. Anderson reached over and tousled Kate's hair. "Try not to worry about Biscuit," he said. "He has to be around here somewhere. You know we'll do all we can to find him."

Kate nodded.

"We're going to get something to eat, and we'll meet

you back here in time for the show. How does that sound?" he continued.

Elizabeth nodded, then watched her parents and James head toward a cluster of hamburger and hot dog stands.

"I'm not sure how much we should tell them," she said to Kate.

"Tell them everything," she said. "At this point, we can use all the help we can get."

The girls went to the Fiesta Noche stage and found Gary.

"Can we do anything to help set up?" Elizabeth asked.

Gary looked at Kate compassionately, then answered Elizabeth. "Why don't you do the usual—play for the crowd? And Kate, you come with me. I have the perfect job for you." He led Kate to box of black microphone cords. "These have gotten all tangled. Could you please straighten them out for me, and coil each one neatly?"

Elizabeth smiled. *Perfect. Busywork is exactly what Kate needs right now, to keep her mind occupied.*

Elizabeth sat down at the bench, feeling almost guilty. Everyone else was working, and here she was, getting to do the thing she loved most in the world. She didn't feel guilty enough to question it, though. She played a couple of scales to warm up. Then, she began playing a 1950s rock 'n' roll rhythm that was sure to draw attention. Sure enough, within a few minutes, the seats began to fill with people.

She was surprised when the sound of a bass guitar joined her. Turning, she saw Joe engrossed in the music.

When did he get here? she thought, but continued to play.

Joe continued playing, but discreetly moved directly behind her. "I'm on a break, and I need to get back to the music store. I think I may have found something," he whispered. "Can you and Kate meet me at the store at eight o'clock?"

Keeping her eyes on the crowd, she whispered, "We'll do our best."

After playing a few more measures, Joe set the guitar down and left the stage. Elizabeth continued playing until Gary nodded to her, signaling it was time to begin the mime show. Kate waited for her at the stage door, and together they crossed behind the stage and over the small bridge. They found seats near Elizabeth's parents.

James laughed at the mime clowns. The girls, on the other hand, couldn't concentrate on the show. Kate once again held the tracker in her hand, watching the red dot move slowly in the center of the screen.

Something out of the corner of Elizabeth's eye caught her attention. There, coming around the curve, was the Skipper and his boat of tourists. She elbowed Kate. "Look," Elizabeth whispered.

Kate looked up, and Elizabeth watched the girl's hands clench into tight fists. "What did you do with my dog?" Kate whispered.

The Skipper floated by, his fake smile pasted in place, giving witty, memorized discourse about San Antonio and the history of the Riverwalk. At one point his eyes scanned the crowd, and he seemed to pause on Elizabeth and Kate. His smile faded for just an instant, with something akin to rage—or was that fear?—momentarily taking over his features. The man recovered quickly, pasting on that smile again, and the girls watched him and his boat float out of sight.

The show ended, and the crowd applauded and began to leave. Kate and Elizabeth didn't move. Neither did Elizabeth's parents. What should have been a fun, carefree vacation had turned into a nightmare.

"Okay, girls. Tell us everything," Mr. Anderson said. "Start from the beginning. I have all the time in the world."

Elizabeth took a deep breath, then began pouring out the story. She told him about Joe and the water balloon. She told him about Gilligan and the Skipper, and watching them in some sort of payoff. She told him about the men chasing them, the failed sting operation, about Biscuit's disappearance, the blog threats, and finally, about hearing Biscuit through the pipes.

During Elizabeth's speech, Kate sat watching the tracker. Fat tears splashed on the ground beside her shoes, but she said nothing.

Mr. Anderson sighed. "How in the world, Elizabeth, do you manage to get yourself caught up in these messes? All those years of taking music lessons of every kind. You're supposed to be sitting sweetly in a parlor somewhere, playing your piano. You're not supposed to be out chasing criminals and solving mysteries!"

Elizabeth wasn't sure how to respond, so she said nothing.

Mr. Anderson looked at the tracker in Kate's hand. "What is that?" he asked.

"It's a tracker. This light shows where the Skipper is. We're hoping he will lead us to Biscuit," Kate told him.

He noticed Elizabeth's earpiece and asked, "And what do you have in your ear?"

"Uncle Dan put a bug on the Skipper's steering wheel, so we can hear his conversations."

Mr. Anderson stood to his feet and began pacing.

Elizabeth's mom remained quiet. James was hopping down the stairs, one at a time. He reminded Elizabeth of Tigger.

Finally, Mr. Anderson said, "We're going to call the police, and I'm not letting you girls out of my sight until this thing is taken care of. We're going to have a nice, relaxing evening—perhaps we'll take a carriage ride around the city. And we'll let the police handle it from here." He looked at his daughter, waiting for her response.

"Yes, sir," she said.

He pulled out his cell phone and began dialing.

"Dan, what were you thinking?" he said after a moment. "Helping these girls get mixed up in something like this. What in the world were you thinking?"

He listened for a few moments, then said, "Could you please give me the number to the local police?"

Elizabeth watched her father hang up the phone, and he immediately began dialing another number.

"Uh, Dad?" she interrupted him. "If we go to the police, they may hurt Biscuit."

He stopped dialing and looked at his daughter. "Elizabeth, you'll have to trust me. Sometimes it's best just to let the authorities handle these things."

"Yes, sir," she replied. Then, as an afterthought, she said, "Kate and I were supposed to meet our friend Joe at his job in ten minutes. He works at the music store in the mall. Can we just go tell him we're busy this evening, so he and his friends won't be waiting for us?"

Mr. Anderson thought for a moment and said, "Is this the boy who was playing the guitar with you?"

"Yes, sir."

He looked at Kate, then back at Elizabeth. "Okay, but don't dawdle. Do you know where the horse and buggy depot is?"

Elizabeth nodded.

"Meet us there in twenty minutes. Don't be a minute late, you understand? And stay together!"

"Yes, sir!" the girls said in unison. They dashed for the Riverwalk entrance to the mall. It would have been quicker to use one of the secret passageways Uncle Dan had shown them, but with Elizabeth's father watching, they didn't want to take any chances.

As soon as they were inside the mall, they began to jog. Within minutes, they were in the music shop, but there was no sign of Joe.

Elizabeth approached a young clerk and said, "Excuse me, we're looking for Joe Garcia. Is he still working?"

The clerk gestured to a door that led to the back of the store. "He's back there unloading some boxes. Go on back."

The girls entered through the door and called out, "Hello! Joe, are you back here?"

"Over here," came a voice from the far left corner, and the girls headed that way. They found Joe behind a large drum set.

"You won't believe this," he said. "Remember how we thought Biscuit was on the other end of some maze of pipes?"

The girls nodded.

"Well, we were wrong. Biscuit is on the other side of this wall! Look!" He pointed to a locked door with a tiny window near the top. Elizabeth stretched to see through, and sure enough, there was Biscuit! He was locked in a kennel. He looked like he was sleeping. Poor little thing.

"Kate, I can see him," she said. Then, looking her friend in the eyes, she smiled and said, "God is good."

Joe found a wooden crate and moved it below the window, so Kate could see. "It's Biscuit! I see him! Biscuit, wake up! Here, boy!"

"Shhhh!" Joe told her. "That Gilligan man has been in and out all day. He comes in every time Biscuit starts howling. You don't want to wake him up again!"

"Why didn't you tell me you had found him, when you were at the Fiesta Noche?"

"Because I hadn't found him until about ten minutes ago. I could hear him all day, though, and Gilligan, too, and I knew they were close. But these boxes were piled in front of this door. I didn't even know there was a door here," Joe told them.

Suddenly, Biscuit's howling cut through the air like a knife. Apparently, he had heard Kate's voice.

Standing on the box again, Kate called out, "Hey, boy! It's okay. I'm here. We're gonna figure out a way to—" She stopped in mid-sentence. Her eyes grew wide, and her face grew pale. Finally, she whispered. "It's—it's him! And he saw me!"

Within moments, the door in front of them was shaking, and they heard the man's voice yelling, "Hey! Get out of here! You kids will be sorry!" Then the lock in the door began to turn.

The three of them looked at each other, but it was Elizabeth who spoke. "We'd better get out of here!"

Captured!

The three of them took off through the storeroom, into the store, barely missing keyboards and drum sets, and into the mall.

"This way," Joe called, and the girls followed. "I'll explain to my boss later."

They ran into a bath store and hid behind a large shelf filled with towels and large bottles of bubble bath. Out of breath, they stood panting and peeking through the cracks in the shelving.

"There he is," whispered Elizabeth, spotting the man. He was looking this way and that, trying to figure out where they had gone. Finally, he moved out of sight, to the left of the bath store.

"I have to go back and get Biscuit," whispered Kate.

"But what if he catches us?" Elizabeth asked.

"It doesn't matter," Kate responded. "If we don't go back and get him now, there's no telling what will happen to him."

"She's right," whispered Joe. "The door is probably still

unlocked. If we're going to do it, we need to do it now."

The three of them carefully stepped from behind the shelf and looked around. There was no sign of Gilligan. They dashed back to the music store, where the clerk gave them a frustrated look. "Joe, what do you think you're doing? And who was that old guy who came crashing through here?"

"Sorry, Harry," Joe called. "I'll explain later, and I'll clean up the mess, I promise!"

Kate led the way back through the storeroom. Biscuit's howls were getting louder. The girl pushed her way through the instruments, squeezing between boxes, until she got to the door. Sure enough, it opened easily. "Biscuit!" she called out.

Elizabeth tried to help her open the kennel door, but it was stuck. In the process, she bumped the tiny speaker, which had been muted. Suddenly, they heard the Skipper's voice. It sounded like he was talking on his cell phone.

"What do you mean, they've found the hideout? How could a bunch of kids—never mind. I'm on my way. You keep looking for them. Where are you now?"

There was static, and Elizabeth looked at the tracker clipped to Kate's belt loop. The Skipper's dot was getting closer. . . .

The Skipper's voice came over the tiny speaker again as the three of them continued to struggle with the kennel door. "You're what? Get back to the hideout, you big dope!

Those kids want the dog. That's where they'll go! I'll be right there."

"We've got to get out of here," said Elizabeth.

"Here, let me have the kennel," said Joe. He grabbed the bulky metal cage with both arms and said, "Go! I have Biscuit!"

Just as they were about to move back through the door into the music storeroom, their passage was blocked.

"Going somewhere?" asked Gilligan. The three kids stopped, frozen in their tracks.

God, help us out of here! prayed Elizabeth.

"This way!" shouted Joe as he motioned to a door at the back of the room. It obviously led to the Riverwalk.

Suddenly, that door banged open, and the Skipper loomed in the doorway.

"Well, now," he snarled, "what do we have here?"

The two men began pressing in. Biscuit growled from his kennel, and the Skipper yelled at Kate, "Make your dog be quiet!"

Oh, God, please help us!

Harry appeared in the doorway to the storeroom. "Hey, what's going on here?" the young man asked.

The two men turned to look, and Joe took advantage of the moment by barreling into Gilligan with Biscuit's kennel.

"Run!" Joe yelled.

The crash forced the kennel door open, and Biscuit leapt from the cage, biting Gilligan on the ankle.

"Ow! Get off me, you little mutt!" the man cried.

Elizabeth and Kate sprang through the door.

"Come on, boy!" Kate yelled.

Biscuit followed his beloved owner. Crashing and banging all the way, the girls ran past Harry, through the storeroom, and into the mall.

"This way!" Elizabeth called, remembering the horse depot. She didn't know if the men were following, but she knew where to find safety, and she ran for her father.

"Stop those kids!" the Skipper yelled.

Mall shoppers turned to watch as the two girls and the dog ran with the Skipper wheezing behind them, and Gilligan limping behind him.

Out the mall doors they went, onto the sidewalk. The Texas heat was a startling contrast to the air-conditioned mall. It was difficult for the girls to see in the dusky gray of the evening. Making sure Kate was still close, Elizabeth yelled, "Follow me!"

She could see her father ahead, right in front of the horse depot, paying the carriage driver. A police officer stood behind him, notepad in hand.

"Dad!" Elizabeth yelled, and he looked up.

They were almost home free when Kate tripped. The Skipper, unaware of his audience, caught up with her and grabbed her by the arm. "I've got you now, you little—"

Biscuit lunged at the man, attacking him, growling, biting, barking. . . . The man did all he could to free himself of the ferocious dog. Then, seeing Mr. Anderson and the police officer running toward him, he grabbed Biscuit and ran down a narrow alley leading back to the Riverwalk.

By this time, Gilligan had caught up with them. Confused, he followed his leader.

There they went, the Skipper with Biscuit clamped tightly to his arm, the injured Gilligan, Elizabeth, Kate, Mr. Anderson, the police officer, and bringing up the rear, Joe. As they reached the other end of the alley, the crowds parted. The Skipper, who was still struggling with Biscuit, was running faster than his out-of-shape body could handle. He failed to slow down in time to gain his balance, and plunged right into the river.

"Don't worry, boss! I'll save you!" called Gilligan, and jumped in after his leader. Then, realizing he was being pursued by the police, he tried to swim to the other side.

Biscuit, finally loose of his kidnapper, swam to the edge and climbed out. Kate scooped the sopping dog into her arms.

"Biscuit! You're safe! I thought I'd never see you again!"

Biscuit rewarded her with slobbery kisses all over her face, knocking her glasses askew.

By this time, the officer had called for backup, and more police officers were starting to arrive. The girls watched as one of them pulled the Skipper out of the water and handcuffed him. Another officer waited for Gilligan on the other side.

Mr. Anderson placed his hands on either side of his

daughter's face, examining her, making sure she was really okay.

"Do I even want to know what just happened here?" he asked.

Elizabeth threw her arms around her father's neck and said, "I love you, Daddy!"

● — ● — ●

An hour later, the horse trotted along at a slow pace, pulling the eight-passenger carriage through the streets of San Antonio. Mr. and Mrs. Anderson sat facing the front, along with James, Kate, and Biscuit. Elizabeth, Joe, Maria, and Pedro faced the back.

"This is cool," said Maria. "Thank you, Mr. Anderson, for letting us come along."

"My pleasure," said Mr. Anderson. "Any friend of Elizabeth's is a friend of mine."

"I can't believe there was actually a reward for those guys," Joe said. "Did you hear the officer say they were wanted for fraud, theft, and vandalism in three states?"

"Yes," Mr. Anderson answered. "Apparently, they've tried before to start a business and destroy the competition. You'd think by now they'd realize they can't destroy competition by force. You all helped to solve a federal case."

"Man, Joe." Pedro shook his head. "I guess you'd better think twice next time, before you try to get a girl's attention by dropping a water balloon on her head!"

Elizabeth gasped. "You said that was an accident, that

you weren't aiming for me!"

Joe looked embarrassed, and suddenly, so did Elizabeth. Everyone laughed. Kate took pity on her friend and changed the subject. "When we divide the reward money five ways, we each get four hundred dollars. That's a lot of money! What will you guys do with your money?"

"Drums!" called Pedro.

"Bass guitar!" said Joe.

Maria looked thoughtful. "I may open a savings account. I've always wanted to go to college, and that will be a nice start," she said.

Elizabeth looked thoughtful. "I'm not sure what I'll do with the money yet. I may use it to go to a piano competition in Nashville. I've always wanted to see Tinsel Town."

"I won't have any problem spending my money on gadgets," said Kate.

"Well, whatever you spend your money on," said Mrs. Anderson, "you've earned it. I'm glad those men are finally behind bars."

Everyone agreed, and the carriage fell silent for a time as they listened to the clip-clopping of the horse and enjoyed the San Antonio city lights.

● — ● — ●

The next morning, Elizabeth was putting the finishing touches on her French braid when the phone rang. It was Uncle Dan.

"Congratulations, detective," he told her.

"Thanks, Uncle Dan. We couldn't have found Biscuit without your help," she answered. "You really should let us give you part of the money."

"Oh, I don't know about that. You've got some pretty good sleuthing skills, and I had nothing to do with that. Are you and Kate about ready to come downstairs?" he asked.

"Yes, sir. Why? Did you need me to bring you something?"

"Yes. Bring Biscuit," he answered, and hung up the phone.

Elizabeth wondered about his cryptic instructions. "Kate, Uncle Dan wants us to bring Biscuit with us."

"That's strange. We always bring him. Why would he call to tell us that?" Kate questioned.

Elizabeth shrugged. "I don't know, but we need to get going anyway."

Kate clipped Biscuit's leash to his collar, and he snorted.

"I know you don't like this leash, boy, but I'm not taking any chances." She gave her dog a hug, scooped him into her arms, and followed Elizabeth out the door.

When the elevator doors opened to the lobby, Uncle Dan was waiting for him. Next to him was Captain Lyndel, holding a huge bone in his hand. Tied around the bone was a big, red bow.

"Good morning," the man greeted. "I wanted to stop by and say thanks for all your help. Because of you, my business will be back on track in no time. I'm sorry Biscuit was kidnapped in the process."

Kate set Biscuit on the floor, and the man placed the bone in front of him. They laughed as Biscuit tried, unsuccessfully, to get his tiny jaws around the bone.

"Here are some other treats for him," the man said, holding out a large gift bag. "There might be a few things in there for you girls, too. Go ahead. Open it."

The girls thanked the man, and peeked into the bag. Sure enough, along with the squeaky toys and bacon-flavored treats, were a couple of furry pink journals and glittery ink pens. There was also a certificate for each of them, offering free River City Cruise rides for life.

"Cool! Thank you so much!" the girls told the man, and Uncle Dan smiled proudly.

"It's my pleasure, girls. I only wish I could do more for you. You saved my business—you and those friends of yours. Would you give them these for me?" He held out three more certificates.

"Certainly," Elizabeth said. "I know they'll be excited to have these. Thank you."

The man tipped his hat and bid them good-bye. Biscuit wagged his tail and barked after the man, then went back to his oversized bone.

"Have I told you I'm proud of you?" Uncle Dan asked Elizabeth.

"The feeling is mutual," she replied, hugging her favorite uncle.

● — ● — ●

Elizabeth sat across from little Annie at Bible Camp, helping the kids with their craft projects. She was so glad that James had befriended the lonely girl. While some of the other children seemed alarmed about Annie's large birthmark, James didn't seem to notice. He shared his crayons and complimented Annie's picture. Without warning, Elizabeth hugged her brother from behind, placing a kiss on top of his head.

"Hey, cut that out!" he fussed, wiping the place where she had kissed him. She laughed, then looked up to see Mr. Adams walking toward them. His timing was perfect. Annie's mother would be here any minute to pick up her daughter.

"Hello, Elizabeth! I believe you had someone for me to meet," he said with a smile.

"Yes, sir. I'll introduce you to everyone." Quickly she named each child sitting at the table, ending with, "And this is Annie."

The man knelt in front of Annie, who hid her face with her curls. "Hello, Annie. It's very nice to meet you."

Annie's mother appeared, and Elizabeth waved to her. "Hello, Mrs. Lopez. I'd like you to meet Mr. Adams. He represents the local Kiwanis Club, and I think he wants to talk to you about something."

The man stood and smiled at the woman.

"That's quite a little girl you have," he told the woman.

"I understand she needs surgery. Our organization would like to help. It may take us a while to raise the money we need, but we'd like to take care of the surgery, if that's all right with you."

The woman looked confused, then relieved, and then joyful as she listened to Mr. Adams. Elizabeth went to find Kate, who was packing sound equipment.

"It's going to happen. Annie's really going to get the surgery she needs!" Elizabeth told her.

"Yeah, I saw them talking. That's great. And you, know, I've been thinking. . . " Kate paused.

"Yes?" Elizabeth probed, wondering if Kate was thinking the same thing she'd been thinking.

"I just. . ."

"Yeah?" Elizabeth leaned forward in anticipation.

Kate pushed her glasses up on her nose. "Instead of buying gadgets, I think I want to give my reward money to Annie, for her surgery."

Elizabeth threw her arms around her friend, nearly knocking Kate over.

"Whoa, there. Easy, girl." Kate laughed. "You're almost as bad as Biscuit!"

"I wanted to do the same thing, but I didn't want you to feel bad, or feel like you had to give your money!" Elizabeth told her.

Kate nodded. "It would be fun to go a little gadget crazy. But I don't *need* any more gadgets. I have more than

I can play with now. And Dad will keep giving me what his students invent. Annie *needs* that surgery. I think that's what I'm going to do with my money."

"And I don't *need* to go to that piano competition," said Elizabeth.

"Hey, where's the music?" called a voice from the shadows. It was Joe, followed by Pedro and Maria. Joe was holding a brand-new guitar case.

"Yeah, I came to hear a concert!" Maria added.

Elizabeth smiled. It looked like her new musician friend had gotten his wish. "Wow, look at you! Is that a new guitar?"

Joe grinned with pride. "It's used, but it's top of the line." He set the case down, opened it, and pulled out a beautiful guitar. Elizabeth fingered the notches, admiring the workmanship.

"I told my new boss about the reward money. He was impressed that I helped solve a crime and offered to let me take this now. He said I can pay him whenever the reward check comes in."

"So, play something!" Elizabeth urged him, and the boy began to strum the strings.

Pausing, he looked at Elizabeth, then Kate, then back at Elizabeth. "You know, I've really enjoyed the last few days. And it's more than just making new friends and getting to buy a guitar. I think it's. . .it's. . ." He struggled for the right words.

"I think it's God," Elizabeth whispered.

"Yeah, that's it. I've never known people who were so excited about God. I think I want to know more about Him. I'm going to start going to church, and start reading the Bible my mom gave me."

"Me, too," Maria and Pedro chimed.

Elizabeth noticed Gary working on the soundboard nearby. He winked at her.

"Why don't you give us another concert," Gary said. "Pedro, why don't you play the drums? Then, after the concert, I'd like to spend some time with you guys."

Elizabeth smiled, and her heart seemed to dance as she and her new friends began playing. She looked at Kate, who gave her a thumbs-up. She knew exactly what her friend was thinking: *God is good.*

Mrs. Garcia's Tamales

6 cups masa flour
6 cups chicken broth
1 cup corn oil
2 teaspoons salt
1 teaspoon baking powder
2 large chickens (you can use store-bought rotisserie
    chickens)
2 ½ (12 ounce) jars green salsa or tomatillo sauce
25 to 30 corn husks

1. Soak the corn husks in warm water until they're soft.

2. Using a mixer, blend the masa flour, corn oil, salt, baking powder, and the chicken broth to obtain a consistent mixture without lumps.

3. Shred the chicken and marinate in the green salsa or tomatillo sauce.

4. Spread the flour mixture evenly over corn husks, then spread a spoonful of the chicken on top of the flour (masa).

5. Fold sides of the corn husk to center over the masa so that they overlap. Fold the empty part of the husk under to make a seamed package.

6. Place the tamales in a steamer and cook for 35 to 40 minutes, checking every 20 minutes. When the tamale separates easily from the corn husk, it is ready.

Join the Camp Club Girls online!

www.campclubgirls.com

✿ Get to know your favorite Camp Club Girl in the Featured Character section.

✳ Print your own bookmarks to use in your favorite Camp Club Book!

✳ Get the scoop on upcoming adventures!

(Make sure to ask your mom and dad first!)

FOLLOW THE CAMP CLUB GIRLS

Book 1:
Mystery at Discovery Lake
ISBN 978-1-60260-267-0

Book 2:
Sydney's DC Discovery
ISBN 978-1-60260-268-7

Book 3:
McKenzie's Montana Mystery
ISBN 978-1-60260-269-4

Book 4:
Alexis and the
Sacramento Surprise
ISBN 978-1-60260-270-0

Book 5:
Kate's Philadelphia Frenzy
ISBN 978-1-60260-271-7

Book 6:
Bailey's Peoria Problem
ISBN 978-1-60260-272-4

IN ALL THEIR ADVENTURES!

  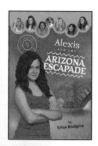

Book 7:
Elizabeth's Amarillo Adventure
ISBN 978-1-60260-290-8

Book 10:
Kate's Vermont Venture
ISBN 978-1-60260-293-9

Book 8:
Sydney's Outer Banks Blast
ISBN 978-1-60260-291-5

Book 11:
McKenzie's Oregon Operation
ISBN 978-1-60260-294-6

Book 9:
Alexis and the Arizona Escapade
ISBN 978-1-60260-292-2

Available wherever books are sold.